Captive Bride

Marjorie J. Hersom

Captive Bride

READERSMAGNET, LLC

Acknowledgments

THIS book could not have come to fruition without the assistance, and the encouragement from my family and friends. My husband, Charles, was supportive and patient. I could not have accomplished this work without his assistance. He listened to each page I completed and read to him, and made constructive suggestions. He served as my research assistant, searching the Internet for clarification, terminology, people, language, everything we thought we needed to bring my story to life. We read books about whaling, who sailed these ships, and where they sailed.

To my children, grandchildren, and great grandchildren, thank you for constantly pushing me with your "Nana, when's the book going to be finished?" To our eldest son, Thomas Hersom, you really were my guide through the maze of our genealogy. Thank you for keeping me on the straight and narrow.

To my good friend Richard Applegate, an author in his own right and a retired newspaperman, who, next to my family, is my biggest supporter. Richard spent many hours editing every word I wrote, questioned, suggested, and encouraged—sometimes in the same breath. Richard constantly encouraged me. Martha, Richard's wife and a very dear friend, stepped in when the book was completed. She corrected and edited it for submission.

The creative writing classes I attended were immensely helpful and encouraging. My teachers and classmates had my back—they reviewed, they corrected, they questioned. A number of them are authors in their own right. I am grateful for their assistance and their encouragement.

The History of the Bonin Islands from the Year 1827 to the Year 1876, the title of a book written by Lionel Berners Cholmondeley, MA, in 1915 served as my bible. This volume has been in my family for a very long time and affectionately called the Green Book. I read and reread this book to learn about the people who played a huge part in making me who I am today. Mr. Cholmondeley, through his acquaintances with the Bonin people, was able to bring Nathaniel Savory to life through the letters written to Mr. Savory by the many sea captains who knew and respected him. Through the letters from the Savory family, the sisters and brothers, I was able to develop the characterizations of all my characters, some factual, some fictional from Mr. Cholmondeley's book. You might say I wore the book out.

It is interesting that since my very early teens, I have loved the story of the Bonin people to whom I have a strong connection. I am so grateful that my dad also loved the story enough to pass it on to us.

The stories my father told at our dinner table were fascinating. Dad mesmerized us with one story after another with our mother injecting more tidbits. I looked forward to our Sunday dinners because there was still more fascinating tales to weave. Today, our family still sits around the dining room table after dinner to share stories, laugh, and just simply enjoy each other.

The year before I began the book, I searched the Internet for information about the Bonin Islands and became acquainted with John Wicke, MD, retired. John was a resource of valuable information about the islands.

John instilled in me the desire to step forward and begin this journey of mine. Through him I found the Webb-Savory branch with a remarkable family history. He was instrumental in opening the door to Dr. Beret Strong whose aunt, Mary Shepardson, assisted in the anthropological study of the ethnicity of the Bonin people. Dr. Wicke, I thank you.

I would be remiss in not acknowledging the writings of Mary Shepardson, who wrote *Bonin Pawns of Power*, an anthropological book of the Bonin Islands, along with her associate Blodwen Hammond who died before their project was completed. I am also grateful to Professor Beret Strong for sharing the book her aunt and Ms. Hammond wrote about the distinct ethnic group of the Bonin Islands.

Finally, yet importantly, I had the pleasure of meeting Jenny Borst, a young creative arts student at Northern Arizona University, who drew a woodcut of Maria and Joaquina at the river. I loved the way she captured the essence of the two girls. Thank you for being part of my story.

Contents

Prologue

THIS is a novel based on historic fact. It is a family saga that takes place between two small North Pacific islands during the mid1800s. It is a true story of a young twenty-two year old adventurer from a small town in Massachusetts who sailed as a crew member to the Sandwich Islands and by happenstance met then joined with four other adventurers who had plans to colonize and plant the British flag on the smallest and unoccupied island named Bonin. And how a very young and beautiful fifteen-year-old girl was tricked onto a ship to see her aunt and is then kidnapped by a violent sailor and taken on a long three-day journey to a place she had never heard of by a man known for his cruelty to women. It is a true story of survival, of faith, and eventually of love and marriage.

Introduction

B ONIN and its adjoining islands were uninhabited, from the mid-1500s up to the early 1800s. The country of Japan was the first to settle on Bonin ("no-man" in Japanese) in the late 1500s. Sometime between 1542 and 1543, a Spanish explorer discovered the islands and gave it the name of Arzobispo. The Spaniard known as Ruy Lopez de Villalobos commanded the exploration. The group never set foot on the island, as their ships were low on freshwater, and they decided to return to the Philippines, never knowing that the new discovery had excellent freshwater and fruits to support their ships.

A Japanese warrior by the name of Ogasawara Sadiyori washed ashore in a storm in 1592. He served under the command of Hideyoshi. For the discovery, the emperor granted a fief in his name, and they became known as the Islands of Ogasawara. This is the name the Japanese call it today. Although the grant was in honor of him, Ogasawara was not happy. He was too far away from the mainland and, after a very short stay, returned to Japan. Once again, the islands became no man's land. It remained uninhabited until the 1800s. These uninhabited islands came under the flags of different countries that sailed around the world exploring shipping routes to the Orient and northern whaling fields.

Bonin came under Japanese rule a second time when the Japanese empire decided to colonize the island. The group of Japanese settlers tried to make the best of living conditions but found that the soil was not good for growing rice, their staple, and life there was too harsh. They returned to Japan, having failed their mission.

In 1827, following the Arrowsmith's chart (in use at that time), a British sloop called the HMS *Blossom* sailed into the large harbor with a complement of 122 men and armed with fifteen guns. They had sailed from England with instructions to assist with the Franklin and Parry Arctic Expedition in the Bering Sea. However, they were unable to make that connection. Captain Beechey, the ship's captain, forced by the wind and sea currents, had to find a safe harbor to anchor and found a land opening that appeared to be promising. The *Blossom* anchored in this magnificent harbor, which Captain Beechey promptly named Port Lloyd after the bishop of Oxford. It informally became British, although no flag was posted.

In 1830 a contingent of twenty Kanakas and five colonists—two British (John Millinchamp and Matteo Mazarro), two Americans (Nathaniel Savory and Aldin Chapin), and one Dane (Charles Johnson)—set out from the Sandwich Islands with the blessings of the British consulate. When the group landed on shore, the two British subjects promptly planted the British flag, announcing to the world this island now belonged to Britain. The group successfully colonized the Bonin, which eventually became a "port o' call" for hundreds of whalers heading to and from the Bering Straits.

Although the Union Jack flew over this small atoll, the British government all but ignored it. Two of the men, John Millinchamp and Matteo Mazarro, British subjects, were responsible for arranging the groups' exploration with the enthusiasm of Richard Charlton, who at that time served as the British consul in Honolulu, the Sandwich Islands.

Mazarro and John Millinchamp were initially appointed by Mr. Richard Charlton to head the group. Mr. Mazarro talked a good game, made a definite impression on the consular, who appointed him the island's first governor. Although given the title, Mazarro did not know how to govern. He in turn appointed Nathaniel

Savory to serve as the magistrate. Savory, well liked and trustworthy, was the man every ship captain went to for assistance and various needs. Port Lloyd became a stopping point for the whalers going and coming from the whaling fields in the Bering Straits.

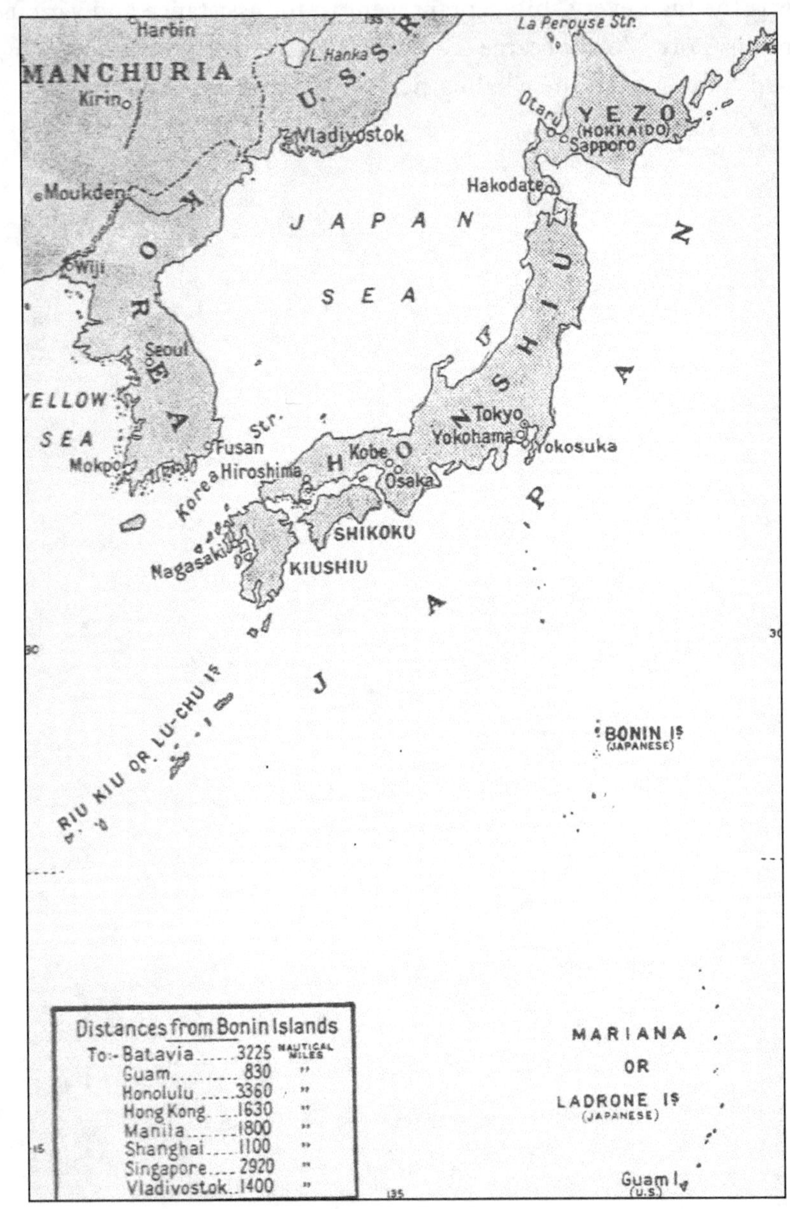

Map showing Japan, Bonin, and Guam

Mag. N.
THE
BONIN ISLANDS
English Miles
0   ½   1   2   3
Kita Jima
Tide Rip Pt
Big Turtle Cove
Eagle Bay
Little Turtle Cove
Winter Turtle Beach
Skunk Pt
NORTH ISLAND
(STAPLETON I.)
(OTOTO JIMA)
Winter Turtle Beach
Big B.
Big Bay Pt
Little Straits Beach
Little Beach
Little Straits Pt
Little Straits
Dick's Stare Hole
Lona B.
HOG ISLAND
(BUCKLAND I.)
(ANI JIMA)
(Capt Pease's Little Goat Island) generally called Pihi Island
Booby
Merry Wilson
Long Beach
LITTLE GOAT I.
Charlie's Little Island
Walker's Bay
Cabbage Beach
Tamura Beach
Tabob Beach
Jack Williams
(Nijenohama)
Hospital B.
Dewils Pt
Hog I. Strait
Toby's Beach
Toby's Beach Pt
Washington B.
Okumura
(Down the Bay)
Long Pt
SANDY BEACH ISLAND
Omura
White Rock
(The other side)
Savory's Pt
Salt Pt
Stiver's Beach
Gold Heart
Joe Kanaka Beach
Welcome Rk
Brava Pk
Brava Pt
N. Stony Beach
S. Stony Beach
PORT LLOYD
Lit & Big Bull B.
Castle Rk
Bill Beach
Ugly Gulch
Black Beach
Goat I. Hd
Susaki
or Blossom Village or Clarkson
Ogiura (Aki)
PEEL Id
Box Beach
Savid's Beach
Rukunui
(CHICHIJIMA)
THE MAIN Id
Deep Bay
Black Beach
White Beach
White Beach
Hump Back Beach Pt
Little Calabash
Middle Bay
Bull Beach
Jinny Beach
Fitton Bay or Tiffin Bay
First B.
KNORR I.
Gold Mine
Gold Mine Pt
Mulberry Bay
Tenoura Pt
Tenoura B.
South East Pt

The Ruse

Joaquina and Maria at the river

THE hot sun quickly evaporated the morning rain, and the steam from the roads rose through the gently swaying coconut trees touched by the balmy breezes of the Pacific. This day in 1843, near the shoreline at the village of Hagatna on the island known as Guam in the Marianas, two teenage girls were busy washing their family's clothes near the mouth of the Hagatna River.

Fifteen-year-old Maria and her seventeen-year-old married aunt, Tita Joaquina, always enjoy this quiet spot on the Hagatna River where large river rocks form a clear pool perfect for washing clothes. Usually, they have the company of other women from the village, but today Joaquina had been anxious to go earlier than usual. Maria soaked and soaped the clothes, while Joaquina rinsed, then slap, slap, slapped each item on a flat rock for deep cleaning. They squeezed each piece and laid the damp clothes out to dry on the rocks and bushes nearby. After completing the laundering, they stripped down to their camisoles and stepped into the pool to bathe and wash their long, flowing black hair.

Although close by, the village was hidden from view by a forest of banyan and coconut trees surrounded by tall shore grass, but sounds could be heard.

Joaquina nervously looked toward the village. Maria stepped out of the water, dried off, and asked, "Tita, is something wrong?"

"Oh no," Joaquina hastily replied as she combed her shiny raven hair, which reached the ground, "I just thought I heard something, probably just the children playing games."

Maria finished getting dressed then helped Joaquina gather some of the clothes that already dried. Being close, Maria knew Joaquina's moods, thinking, *something isn't right. Tita is not herself. What is causing her to seem anxious?*

Shortly thereafter, the sound of voices and heavy footsteps caused both of them to look up. Maria wondered, *what is this? Who are these men?*

Two men appeared in the clearing, both strangers to Maria. One had light brown hair and a large mustache. He smiled and said, "Hafa adai," a greeting in the native Chamorro language.

The other man, dark-skinned and much older than the first man, bowed his head, and said, "Buenos Dias, Senora y Senorita."

Uncomfortable with the intrusion, Maria excused herself to pick up the rest of the drying clothes.

Joaquina responded with a smile, "Hafa adai."

Joaquina's father introduced Millinchamp to her when Millinchamp attended the fiesta in honor of Santa Mariana, the patron saint of Guam, on his visit the month before. Taken by Joaquina's beauty and charm, he paid her a great deal of attention. Flattered by the attention that Millinchamp gave her, she agreed to meet with him as often as they could, and she fell hopelessly in love, as did Millinchamp. During their meetings, they talked of being together, and soon Millinchamp proposed marriage and planned Joaquina's escape from the abuses of her common-law spouse. At that time, he said he would return to Guam in one month and put their plan into motion.

On his return a month later, Joaquina and Millinchamp reunited and put the final touches toward their future. Joaquina shared with him how much she would miss Maria. On hearing this from Joaquina and wanting to please his love, Millinchamp suggested, "Perhaps you can convince your niece to leave with us, Joaquina. Would that make you happy?"

Remembering that conversation regarding Maria, Joaquina knew that John was sincere in his attempt to please her. Nevertheless, Joaquina said, "Oh no, no matter how close we are, Maria would never leave our family, especially leaving without their permission. No, never! I love you so much I would do anything for you, but I know Maria would never leave, never!"

Joaquina then walked over to Maria and asked, "Do you remember Capitan Millinchamp, Maria? He came to the Santa Mariana fiesta on his last trip. Papa invited him to come back when he next returned. He's here to see me before he returns to the Bonins."

"No, I...I do not remember meeting Senor Millinchamp," answered Maria, hesitantly.

Millinchamp, a blue-eyed Englishman of slight build, turned to his friend and introduced him to Joaquina and Maria, saying, "This is my shipmate and friend, Matteo Mazarro, from Genoa. The *Portsmouth* is our schooner moored out in the harbor. We'll be heading back to her after picking up fresh supplies. We sail in the morning for the Bonin Islands, southwest of Japan, with some dry goods and other supplies."

With a broad smile, Millinchamp then looked intently at Joaquina and said, "I will be back before the siesta hour is over." Bowing to both girls, the two men left.

Maria questioned Joaquina, "What is he talking about, Tita?"

Joaquina replied, "Senor Millinchamp wants me to become his wife. He will take me to a place where I will be safe. I am leaving with him. It was foolish of me to become Ramon's wife. Since the day we began living together, he began to beat me, he is an abuser, especially when he drinks…which is all the time."

Joaquina, doing her very best to entice Maria, said, "Now this wonderful man, who is kind and loving, wants to take me with him. I love him, and I know he loves me. You can come with us, Maria, and then we will never be apart."

Shocked but aware of the abuse Joaquina suffered, Maria blustered, "You-you don't even know him! He is old, Joaquina, can't you see that? How can you leave us? Have you told our family?"

Joaquina, ignoring Maria's outburst, answered, "I have prayed to Santa Rita, our patron saint who watches over abused women who live with husbands who beat them and sometimes kill them. Maria, you cannot understand, but please come and see me off. I will tell you more later. Come out to the ship this afternoon, I promise you will be home before the sun sets."

In stunned silence, Maria gathered the partially dried clothing. She turned and looked at Joaquina in dismay as she quickly trudged to the village.

Joaquina ran after her niece and, putting up her hands, stopped her in her tracks and pleaded, "Please, Maria. Don't tell anyone. No one knows but you. They will know tonight after you tell them and the ship is too far away for anyone to do anything about it."

Maria, shaken by what she heard from Joaquina, tried to make sense of what she was told. She tried to answer the questions in her mind, but her youth and innocence got in her way. *How could she just leave like this? Why must I keep this from the family?*

Later that morning, Maria, tears in her eyes, told Joaquina, "I will see you off and say good-bye. I know your mind is made up, but you must tell me more, so I can understand."

Maria was in a colorful skirt and soft cotton overblouse in striking contrast to her silken black hair tied in a thick braid hanging down to her hips. She wrapped a large woven red scarf over her shoulders to protect her from the offshore winds. Arriving at the harbor earlier than expected, she noticed a ship's skiff on the beach. Maria watched the activity of the harbor while waiting for Joaquina to arrive.

Everyone seemed to be too busy to notice this beautiful young girl, except a man coming toward her from the skiff, waving in her direction. As he came closer, she recognized him, thinking, *He is the man I saw with Millinchamp earlier this morning.* A feeling of dread came over her, but she let it pass, giving it no importance.

Senor Mazarro, a middle-aged man, walked slowly toward her, while taking his cap off to wipe his brow. Maria, noticing his brown-black hair streaked with white flying loosely in the breeze, felt a little tense as he approached her.

"Senorita, your *Tia* and Captain Millinchamp are already on board the *Portsmouth.* I was asked to come and get you. Our crew is readying the schooner to sail in the morning. Come." Mazarro, gazing at Maria as she listened to his reason for being there instead of Joaquina, thought, *She is quite beautiful, quite a morsel and so young!*

He smiled at Maria as he rowed the skiff out to the schooner. When they approached the ship, he called up, "Ship's mate Mazarro boarding the *Portsmouth* with a guest, request permission to board!"

Someone responded, "Aye! Aye! Permission granted."

Mazarro stepped up on the side ladder, turned, and gave Maria his hand to assist her.

Once on deck, Maria asked with concern, "Where is Joaquina?"

"Follow me. I will take you to her."

Moving across the main deck and down the companionway, Maria hesitantly followed. The air was dank and smelled of hemp from the heavy ropes coiled in the hold and from other unidentified things. She became even more uncomfortable in this strange setting, wondering, *Where is he taking me? Joaquina must be in another part of this ship.*

Maria began to relax upon seeing light ahead of her. She had never been on a ship this large. Stepping through the doorway, she saw Joaquina waiting. Relieved, Maria ran into her outstretched arms, saying, "Joaquina, I am so relieved to see you, this is such a big ship."

Mazarro excused himself, saying, "If you will excuse me, Senora y Senorita, I must go and help prepare the ship for departure."

Joaquina kept Maria busy with idle words, noticing that Maria hadn't caught on to Mazarro's words about getting the ship ready for departure. Suddenly they heard the shouts of orders to release the ship from its mooring, the sound of men scurrying about preparing the ship for sailing. "Anchors aweigh!" someone shouted.

Hearing the grating sound of the wench being turned to pull up the anchor, Maria jerked herself out of Joaquina's arms and ran to the side of the ship screaming, "No! No! Joaquina! Joaquina! The ship is moving, I have to go back home! Joaquina, what is happening?"

Joaquina answered, "John saw how close you and I were and suggested that you might want to come with us to the Bonin Islands. Of course, I agreed, as you will have a happier life there, and we can be together as always."

Maria, devastated and frightened, cried, "You lied to me! Why? Mama! Papa!"

"The ship began to move slowly off its mooring and into deep waters. Maria screamed, "Mama! Papa! Help me! Help me!"

To her horror, it now was obvious to Maria, a young and naive girl, that this ruse was meant to take her without her consent, and Millinchamp, Mazarro, and Joaquina must have planned this before they met at the river this morning.

Although Millinchamp gave Joaquina the suggestion in good faith, Mazarro had planned a different scene. Instead, the kidnapping set the stage for his lecherous desires and his practical needs for another female companion. Even Joaquina and Millinchamp were duped.

The Capture

L ITTLE did Joaquina know that Mazarro was in on the plan to deceive Maria. Never considering the outcome, Joaquina went along with the plot to get Maria on board the schooner…to spirit her away, so to speak.

It seemed so simple. The three conspirators hadn't counted on Maria's outburst. Oh, they all knew there would be tears and a bit of a tantrum, not the insane drama they witnessed.

Maria ran to the main deck. She ran to the railing, screaming, "The ship is moving. Wait, wait! I must get off! Stop, let me off!" A frantic Maria climbed onto the yardarms, screaming for help, and kept calling for her parents to save her. Seeing Joaquina, she struck at her and anyone who tried to restrain her.

Millinchamp shouted at Mazarro, "Control the girl!" Looking at Joaquina with hard eyes, he said between clenched teeth, "Ye betta get her under control." Finally catching Maria, Mazarro forcibly restrained her.

Although shaken by this outburst, Joaquina helped Mazarro take her to his cabin. Maria, spent from the emotional tirade, fell on the bunk moaning over and over, "Mama, Papa," until she fell asleep.

Joaquina, frightened and remorseful for her part in this deception, stayed close to Maria while she slept. Maria awoke to a sobbing Joaquina and wailed, "Tita…why, why?"

"I am so sorry, Maria, all I wanted was to get away from Ramon. I agreed to help Millinchamp and Mazarro convince you to come with us to their island. I need you to be with me. You and I have been closer than sisters. You are the best part of my family."

Maria looked at Joaquina in shocked silence, casting a disgusted look at her as she thought, *How could she do this to me and my family? I will fight this, I will.*

Many ships from different countries visited the island of Guam to resupply their vessels with fresh fruits, vegetables, and dry goods. Guam, a possession of the Spanish Crown was a perfect stopping-off point for the whalers on their way to the North Pacific and for the English merchantmen moving goods back and forth from China to the Sandwich Islands (Hawaii) and on to Europe. It was not uncommon for young beautiful girls to disappear, never to be seen again. Human trafficking brought a lot of money to the unscrupulous ship captains who captured men and women. They were considered goods to trade or sell. Guam was a perfect place to steal titian-haired innocent young girls to sell to Chinese brothels.

Being approximately nine hundred miles southwest of the Bonins, Guam was one of the islands the *Portsmouth* regularly stopped at on her way to the Bonins.

Once the work of setting sail was accomplished, Mazarro entered the cabin and excused Joaquina. "Ye can go now. She be awright here." Joaquina hesitated for a moment then left.

At first, Mazarro stood over Maria, just staring at her. Then he sat on the bunk and began to caress her softly. Maria, shrugging her shoulders, moved farther into the bunk away from his caress. Frightened by his presence, she cowered deeper against the wall, angering him. Grabbing Maria by the leg and arm, he pulled her up into his face and through tightened lips said, "My dear, git used to me. Ye be mine now, and 'tis nothing ye can do about it!"

Maria struggled, determined to free herself, but Mazarro, strong for a man of his age, threw her back on the bunk, tore off her skirt, and roughly entered her. Maria screamed in pain. Mazarro clamped his hand over her mouth and whispered hoarsely, "It will do you no good, me dear, no one will come in here, no one!" She struggled until she had no more energy to fight back, folded, and finally gave up.

After traveling three days and four nights, Maria was numb. Each night and day was the same to her. She would not fight back. She would just lie there. Throughout the trip, she never left the cabin, she could not eat, and she spoke to no one. She could no longer trust Joaquina. Mazarro liked it that way. He carried on as if nothing was out of the ordinary, and he reasoned that Maria was just young and naive, thinking, *she'll come around and even come ta like it, if she knows what's good fo' her. She be grateful.*

Maria prayed for death. She was in pain; every part of her body hurt. She had no one! Her mind wandered. *Would dying be easier? What have I done to deserve this treatment? Would Papa and the rest of my family be searching for me and Joaquina?*

A feeling of shame swept over her...a deep, deep shame, for what this awful man, Mazarro, did to her. She was deeply scarred because of what happened. Maria knew she could never forgive her aunt.

The Rape

MARIA'S body begged for mercy. Mazarro's assault was painful and constant. Weakened from her violent vomiting, her body, her nerves were on the breaking point. She hurt everywhere, physically and emotionally. Still nauseous from being seasick, she begged to die. *How much more can I take,* she wondered. She was sticky and dirty from sweat and blood. A young innocent little girl just three days before, she knew in her heart if she survived this torment, she would never return to her former self. Her life had changed.

The sea was rough and relentless. The *Portsmouth* rose and fell hard with each surge of the ocean, rolling back and forth each time a gigantic wave would hit. The up and down movement of the ship, and the smells in the closed room, made Maria horribly seasick.

She prayed, *Dear heavenly Father, what have I done to deserve this? I have been a good daughter. Please, dear Father, have mercy on me. Give me the strength to endure all that's happening to me!*

Shouting from somewhere on the ship caught Maria's attention. As the wind subsided, the rocking back and forth lessened. Hearing "Land ahoy!" she slowly and painfully sat up. *Where are we? What is going to happen now?*

View of harbor

Activity on board the *Portsmouth* picked up. All hands prepared for arrival into Port Lloyd, their destination and homeport known as Yankee-town. A canoe appeared at the starboard side of the ship. Coming alongside, the man in the canoe laid his oars down and announced his name as Harry, the harbor pilot. The canoe was hoisted up on deck along with Harry who would guide the *Portsmouth* safely through the volcanic rock and the coral outcropping to safe anchorage.

The coxswain shouted, "Ready on the winches, come about!" The harbor pilot stood by the coxswain, ready to assist the safe anchoring of the ship.

Maria, although apprehensive as to what lay ahead, began to feel things were about to change. Mazarro entered the quarters saying, "We have arrived at our port. Ye'll stay here until I have completed mooring the ship. Do not leave this cabin. We will go ashore last."

Afraid of Mazarro, Maria followed his orders thinking, *what else can I do?* She remained in Mazarro's cabin until the business of the ship was finished.

First, the passengers were lowered to the skiffs below and rowed to shore; then the supplies, flour, rice, chicks, grain, and dry goods. Maria could hear happy greetings for the few passengers being met by relatives on shore.

The wind kicked up as night fell, and it was chilly. Maria tried to dress herself with the clothing ripped so violently from her body. She was chilled to the bone. Held captive in a cool, closed, and stuffy cabin, she hadn't smelled the fragrance of the fresh sea air for several days. And this girl who always took a daily bath had not been near a washbasin. Her hair was matted from sweat and blood, her body sore, and sticky; she was miserable. In spite of this, something in her stirred, and she decided to survive. *But it will be my way*, she thought. Maria's pride and dignity wouldn't allow her to be victimized anymore. She wouldn't let this situation destroy her. She knew she must rely on her strength and cunning if she was to survive.

Before leaving the *Portsmouth*, Millinchamp approached Mazarro and lectured him, "Keepin' Maria a slave would be a blemish on our small settlement here in Yankeetown. I advise ye to tread lightly, as the salts…as bad as they come don't like how ye worked the lass over. Ye have to know how hated ye are now with me crew and me friends in Yankeetown. Ye will be further scorned ashore when the islanders hear how ye handled Maria."

Pacing back and forth on the deck, Millinchamp continued, "This lass comes from a powerful family, and salts do a lot of talkin' when they get to port an' hoist a few. Ye best be watchin' yer backside as well."

While rowing toward shore, Mazarro thought about the warning from the captain. *I can take care of me own business. Hell, who made Millinchamp me keeper?*

Matteo Mazarro, often called Matthew, scrutinized Maria and noticed something different, something that wasn't there before. He could see her discomfort, and it was obvious she needed a bath and a good comb. What he saw was a young girl no longer cowering in fear. Looking at her closer, he saw a proud, young partially naked girl, her breasts and body barely covered. There she sat. Her head held high and her shoulders back. *By damn, ye'd think she was royalty,* Mazarro thought. *There she sits all high and mighty. What can this pretty face have up her sleeve? This little beauty ain't goin' ta be easy ta break.*

Yankeetown

MAZARRO pulled the skiff onshore and secured it. Maria wearily stepped from the skiff and trudged to shore. Looking around, she observed her surroundings for the first time and felt strange to be so far away from her home. She felt lost, hopeless, wondering, what is going to happen to her.

From the corner of her eye, although it was dusk, she could make out a large school of shimmering green turtles swimming about in the bay…quite a sight. Twilight touched the island. In the waning light, one could see the silhouette of three hills standing guard over the harbor, as they had since the first volcanic eruption eons ago.

A short distance from their docking spot, Maria eyed the thatched houses scattered over the shoreline. She would soon learn these houses were part of the village the Kanakas established for themselves. However, as the sky darkened, she could barely see the road leading to the village.

Thatched shanties near shoreline

She heard voices drifting toward them. People carrying torches were parading down toward the shore, excited to see the *Portsmouth*'s arrival. The small population of Yankeetown always looked forward to the arrival of the merchant ships and made the arrival festive.

Each member of the town looked forward to something—maybe a long-lost friend, a returning child, or mail from a faraway place.

Seeing all this for the first time in her life, Maria pondered, *what does this mean? It must be their tradition to welcome each ship that sails into port. How nice. I hope no one notices me.*

She covered herself even more with what little clothing she wore.

Impatient, Mazarro called her to follow, not wanting to answer the local citizens' questions about Maria. She slowly turned to leave the port and saw Joaquina and Millinchamp moving away in a rickshaw-like cart. Joaquina waved, but Maria turned her head the other way. Weak from her three days of isolation at sea, she followed slowly.

Mazarro commissioned a cart to carry them up to his house above the main part of Yankeetown. His bungalow situated outside of the boundaries of the town was on a bluff overlooking the southernmost tip of the bay. It sat away from the main town and off the main road.

Arriving at the small house, Mazarro jumped off the cart and motioned for Maria to follow. The driver assisted her off the cart and left as soon as Mazarro paid him. Maria stood where she left the cart, not moving. Mazarro shouted at her to follow him, but she stood there, as if glued to the road. He turned and started to go after her but stopped. Maria stared defiantly at him. He stopped, puzzled by her demeanor. Something told him to go no further.

Hearing a rustling sound, Maria turned just as a young woman exited the house. Mazarro nodded a dismissal to her, and she scurried down the hill. He stepped aside as Maria moved toward the house wondering, *what is this? What can I make of all this? Is this where I will stay? Will I ever, ever be free? Heavenly Father, please give me the strength, the will to survive. Please guide my way.*

<h1 style="text-align:center">Maria Meets Hanna</h1>

Maria slowly followed Mazarro into his shanty. She stood in the middle of the room and shuddered. Twilight filtered into the room from a dirty glass-paned window. What she saw made her cringe—an unmade lumpy, dingy mattress with yellowed sheets. In a corner, she noted a well-traveled steamer trunk that served as a table. A chipped blue-enameled washbasin sat precariously on top. Against the opposite wall stood a rickety table and a filthy green chair with all the cane strapping torn. An out-of-place ornate armoire stood against another wall, so big it gave one the feeling that the room would tip over. The room was small, cluttered, and uninviting.

She didn't even know the day of the week. Suddenly she began to grasp the dire circumstances she was in. In a flash, her life changed. The life she knew no longer existed. Saddened by this, she thought, *Mama and Papa must be searching for me. Do they have any idea of my fate? Are they searching for Joaquina too? Do they know that this is something Joaquina planned? How could they? I was fooled too.*

What is that smell? A peculiar odor permeated throughout the shanty. Maria felt queasy. *That smell could be causing my upset stomach. Being weak from my ordeal at sea and unable to eat could be the reason for such discomfort. I should be feeling better with fresh air and on land again, but that smell isn't helping. Now that we are on land, would my family find me here? I don't even know where I am. How could they?*

Mazarro startled Maria out of her reverie. "Ye'll be livin' here from now on, so git used to it. Ye'll be mine to do what me wants with you an there ain't nobody goin' ta stop me, nobody. Ye be me slave girl, ye be takin' good care of me as long as I wantcha."

Too tired, too weak to respond, Maria couldn't comprehend what he was saying. *Why did this man take me?* She had no idea how many hundreds of miles she was from her homeland and her family. *What else could happen?* Tears flowed down her face as she sobbed and sobbed, and it did not sit well with Mazarro.

One thing she was certain, she loathed this awful man for what he did to her. In her heart she knew, no matter what her circumstances, she would hate this person as long as she lived.

Mazarro pushed Maria toward the bed. She stumbled a bit but held her ground. Like a cornered animal, she showed her fangs. She swung around quickly and pushed him back. As small as she was, she prepared for battle. Mazarro was startled by her aggressiveness, but only for a moment. He hit her with tremendous force, knocking her across the room, as if she were a rag doll.

With what strength she had left, she moved up on her knees then, holding on to the front of the steamer trunk, pulled herself up. She stood, weaving a little, trying to regain her balance. Mazarro was angered at her audacity to stand as if to challenge him. Again, he hit her with such force, it knocked her out. Swearing at her unconscious form, he stepped over her and stormed out of the shanty.

The young woman, who earlier slipped out of the shanty upon Maria's arrival, remained a short distance away and witnessed the fight. She watched as Mazarro stomped off to cool his anger in Yankeetown. She knew his habit of drinking and passing out. Taking a chance with that knowledge and her experiences with his violence, she knew that Mazarro's new girl was in trouble and needed help.

The girl, named Hanna, ran home excitedly shouting, "Mama, Mama Henrietta!"

"Wat you want, Hanna, wat da mattah? Wat you need?"

Telling Mama Henrietta what she had seen, she exclaimed, "Dat girl need hep now!"

Mama Henrietta commanded, "Go back, Hanna. Take sum cloth an' herbs an' liniment to rub on wounds. Mama come afta soon."

The room was dark except for a wide ribbon of moonlight coming through. Familiar with the room's layout, Hanna knew where the kerosene lantern stood. After lighting the wick, she could hear the labored breathing of Maria.

Hanna moved into action. From the rain barrel outside, she filled a blue pitcher using a small ladle. Returning to Maria, she used the cloth she brought from home to gently wash Maria's face. The blood was flowing from her nose and head. Her face was beginning to swell from Mazarro's last big punch that knocked her out. Slowly regaining consciousness, in pain and further weakened from Mazarro's beating, Maria looked at the girl and nodded her head thank-you, grateful for this person's kindness.

"Who are you?" Maria asked in a weakened voice.

"Shhh, my name, Hanna" was the tender reply.

"How did you know I needed help?" Maria asked.

"Hanna watch nearby, I heah Mazarro yellin' an' hit you like he hit stubborn animal. You give heem hard time, you one tough wahine. Mazarro no good…all Bonin peopo know he berry bad man. Who are you, why you wid him?" Hanna asked.

In a weak voice, she said, "My name is Maria del los Santos y Castro. That man took me from my home on the island of Guam," she replied. "Where are we?"

"Hanna liv heah on Bonin Island now, but Ponape Island weah I be born. Mazarro he steal me an' me mudder, an' many odda womin, den take all us berry long way. We stop one time an' all da womin' 'cept me go to a cheenaman, an' dey say no, no for, Hanna no good for um."

"How did you come here, Hanna?" Maria asked.

"Oh, dat Mazarro, da one who brings you, he brings me heah too. He berry bad man. No mo' talks. You need eat. I bring. You wait heah. I be back, Maria, okay?" Hanna left.

Gone only a few minutes, Hanna returned with some fruit, hardtack, and a bowl of fish soup. Maria could only take a sip of the soup, her stomach fighting her all the way.

"Walk slow wid Hanna, she show you latrine, okay?" Maria obliged, struggling to walk upright.

Maria and Hanna

MARIA'S ordeal didn't end with her first night in Yankeetown. It was just beginning. The feeling of queasiness, the bouts of crying, the lack of energy, worsened. She felt as if the nightmare would never end, but it did.

Her life had changed from being a young, naive fifteen-year-old to scrappy survivor—victim of kidnapping, brutal rape, and constant beatings. She was no longer the fifteen-year-old girl stolen less than a week before from the island of Guam.

Mazarro, losing patience with her on a daily basis, thought, *she shoulda give up by now, 'tis goin' on a week since the* Portsmouth *sailed from Guam. She fights me tooth and nail every time I come near her. Dis girl don't give an inch, like a little she-cat, I have scratch marks and teeth bites to prove it. One hellava fighter she be. When I git me way, she'll do anything I order. This little tiger will learn her place here, gotta show her who da boss is. She's me own as long as I want her, by damn!*

That night when Mazarro had fallen asleep, Maria stared at him. Afraid that he might awaken and grab her again, she cautiously peered at her attacker's face. She never really looked at him before. She always had her eyes closed. The moonlight coming through the window gave his face a strange glow. The evil he projected while awake even showed while he slept, causing a shiver to run up her spine.

He is not a young person. He is as old as my grandfathers must be. Mazarro's face is like leather and has many deep valleys. His body is small in stature and weathered. He is much older than my father. Who is he? The people I know don't show evil in their faces when they sleep.

It was getting daylight when Maria limped quietly out of the shanty and moved slowly and painfully toward the privy, still hurting from being battered about from her recent confrontation with Mazarro. Approaching the privy, she heard a voice softly call her name. It was Hanna. Maria smiled at her in recognition, still grateful for her help earlier that night.

Hanna put her fingers to her mouth and said, "Shhhh! Hanna tell Henrietta what Mazarro do. She pretty hot mad, he bad man, Maria. Ye walk slow by heem." Holding her head with both hands and shaking it back and forth, she added, "Ay yii, Mama Henrietta say, he so bad he can keel you and no care. Ye do what he say. Time will take heem, an' ye will still be liv'. Ye must do this to save yer life, Mama says. She knows 'tis not easy, but ye must."

Maria listened intently as Hanna continued, "We be here ta help ye, okay, Maria? Mama send eggs, salt pork, yams, turtle meat, fish, and pineapple to help ye take care of yer duty. Ye cook, Maria? If no, ye must learn, I hep you. I go now."

Maria had no idea what grew here, what the people ate, not a thing about this place. However, the items that Mama Henrietta gave her were familiar foods. She knew how to prepare the fish and the fruit. This would be easy. What lay ahead was the challenge.

Maria, surprised to hear concern in Hanna's voice and the message she brought from Mama Henrietta, silently prayed.

What do I do now, dear Father? Do I listen and take their concerns seriously? I have not been a good daughter to you, and I would understand if you do not answer. I am but a speck in this vast place. Father, there are so many more who call out to you, but I need your help, Father. Please help me. Oh, and, Father, please bless my new friend, Hanna, and her mother, Mama Henrietta. They have been so kind to me. Now that there is light, I will be able to see more and do what needs to be done to save my life. In the name of your son, Father.

She shivered from fear of what lay ahead. In spite of her bruised body and mind, she decided to follow the simple instructions

Hanna had related from Mama Henrietta, thinking, *I will do what Mazarro asks even though I hate and fear him, maybe this will buy me time.*

As she headed toward the shanty, Mazarro awakened and bellowed, "Maariiaa!"

She slackened her pace when she heard his terrible voice. Taking a deep breath, she hurried up to the shack, answering, "Yes, I am here."

Maria's Wrath

MAZARRO stood with feet apart and hands on his hips, ready for another battle. Thrown off course by Maria's submissive response, he gruffly asked, "Where ya been?"

Maria stepped into the room, carrying the basket from Mama Henrietta. Setting the basket down, she asked Mazarro for cooking pots. Her body, painfully sore from the beating he inflicted the night before, caused her to move about slowly as she answered, "Been to the privy. When I came out, this girl gave me the basket from Mama Henrietta."

"Mama Henrietta, Humph! Wimmin!" Once again, Mazarro noted this change in Maria…strength…something. He left the shanty and headed for the privy.

Looking around the room, Maria cringed at the filth. Before she would cook anything, she would have to clean up this part of the room first. Giving the area a quick cleaning, she set about preparing a fire in the small wood stove outside and began cooking the meal, her first in captivity.

How many of these meals will I cook before I am found? she wondered.

Mazarro returned to find food ready. The pineapple was cleaned and sliced, and the yams smelled wonderful as they baked in the wood fire. Maria found the tea and sugar but had no milk. Watching Maria as she prepared the meal, he noticed how slowly she moved about.

"Looks like me needs to capture a female goat with a kid souse we kin have milk, right, Maria?"

She did not acknowledge his remark.

Mazarro, feeling full and comfortable after he ate, decided he needed Maria in his bed. He reached for her arm to draw her to him, but Maria jerked her arm away, moved toward the door, and stood her ground.

Startled by her action, he reached for her again. Maria stood, her back straight. She moved into a fighter's stance and growled, "No! No more, Mazarro, I will not let you hurt me and hurt me. If I have to remain here with you, then you treat me better. I have done nothing to deserve the beatings and pain you have inflicted on me. You are mean, and you think you can scare me into doing what you want. Well, I have news for you."

Stunned by this outburst, Mazarro lunged for her again, but she picked up the machete lying nearby, a familiar tool and one she knew how to use well. Holding it to defend herself, she whipped it around so aggressively that Mazarro jumped backward for fear of being cut. He was unaware of Maria's skill with the knife.

"Put dat machete down, Maria, put it down!"

No! Don't even try to take this away from me, Mazarro…don't even try."

Dis little she-cat means business, nevah evah met or seen no other womin who had dis much scrap in 'er.

"Ahright, ahright, jus' put it down. Best I leave now and check out dah ship, and see if the crew is doin' dea job. Be back, Maria, I be back."

Mama Henrietta musta put a spell on me girl, that's what got into 'er, I swear! Gonna keep Mama Henrietta far away.

Happy to see him leave but still not ready to relax on the chance he would use trickery and take her by surprise, Maria held on to the knife. Deep inside her, a will to survive had kicked in, and she was ready no matter what.

He will be back, but on my terms. We will see who has the upper hand, we will see!

A New Day

Proud of herself for standing up to Mazarro, Maria realized that her new life would fare better than she imagined just a few days ago. She no longer was afraid of Mazarro and his bad temper.

Shortly thereafter, Mazarro left. With a big sigh of relief, Maria looked around for something to cover her body. Her clothing, what little she had, was literally like rags.

The last time I bathed and washed my hair was the day Mazarro took me. It's been almost a week or more. I have never let a day go by without a bath. This won't do. I need to find a place to bathe. I must smell awful. How can I keep my dignity? Papa always told us that no matter where we find ourselves, good or bad, we must keep our faith and our dignity, and it will carry us through. Dear Papa, I would rather be home with you than be here, will dignity matter? No one knows where I am, so I must be strong. I must hold on and never give in.

Rummaging through the armoire, dust flying everywhere, she had a sneezing fit. Between sneezes, Maria managed to find several items of clothing. *Women's clothing, hmmm, I wonder who wore these. There are just a few, and none will fit right now, but I could cut them to fit me.*

She quickly tidied up the room and cleaned the cooking area. She took the dress she'd found and went in search of a place to bathe, a place to wash her clothes, and something to make a broom. Stepping outside, she was able to take in her surroundings for the first time.

Maria's view of harbor from the cabin

Oh, how beautiful, it's so green. It is almost as beautiful as Guam. I don't remember seeing any of this when we came into shore. I didn't even notice the beauty when I went to the privy. How could I have missed it? This island is different from Guam. Palm trees with no coconuts, and not many flowers that I can see, at least not here. It is different. One thing, I notice, we are right at the edge of the sea, and the land ends there. Nothing is protected from the typhoons, though it seems. Maybe I am not seeing things clearly. She stood transfixed for a minute or so.

The view from the cabin was in stark contrast to her immediate surroundings. Around the cabin, there was filth, broken glass, half-finished projects, and trash. Not a thing growing. Nevertheless, looking out toward the harbor, everything appeared fresh and clean. The harbor, a sparkling blue, grew darker as the water flowed with the tide toward the open sea. Mazarro's property had a narrow strip of sand where canoes could be hauled up from the sea, after fishing. This prime spot made it easier for launching the canoes either toward the sea or toward the harbor.

Then Maria noticed that this area wasn't as hilly as she had thought. She found a large piece of level land with the remains of a long-neglected garden, which excited her.

Maybe I can grow some corn, green beans, yams, and cabbage here. Until I am found, I may as well help myself survive. How beautiful. This Bonin is not like Guam but certainly has its own beauty. In Guam, I could see the depth of the harbor where a coral reef surrounds and protects the island. The waters around Port Lloyd are a deep green, becoming darker, almost green-black as the water gets farther from shore.

In the distance, she spotted a dark mass coming toward the shore away from the busy harbor. She watched for what seemed a long time. Swimming toward a small cove were hundreds of massive sea turtles. It was amazing to her. The turtles moved as in a dance, gracefully swimming in concert with each other. The closer they swam to shore, the bigger they appeared to be; black, but as they swam closer, their shells were a dark, dark green. These turtles were enormous, and they made no sound except for the lapping waters hitting their flippers as they swam.

When the Bonins were first settled a few years back, the natives approximately twenty-five, five of whom were women, originally came with the five original settlers. They chose to separate themselves from the original five sailors and settled in their own village on the beach away from the others. Henrietta and Hanna lived in this village.

As Maria watched the turtles, Hanna and Mama Henrietta came up from the shore where they lived and greeted her. "Aloha! You feel betta today, maybe?

"Hafa adai," Maria answered. "Much better today, because you and Hanna helped me, you have been so kind, I am so happy to see you."

"Oh, 'tis da Bonin way," Mama Henrietta exclaimed, "tanks. You look for sumting?"

"Si, si, I am looking for a stream, a little cove, or someplace where I can bathe and, yes, even wash clothes. Do you know if there is such a place?"

Mama responded, "On dis plantation dars plenny places fo' you, but we show you bestes one. Hanna, take Maria to da cove nearby weah da fresh wata meets da sea. Maria, dis is weah you find da perfect place to bathe, da wata is sweet and clear, coming from a stream in the mountain above us. No one bauder you der."

Freshwater stream

"Gracias," Maria replied. "And gracias, Mama Henrietta, for the fruit and eggs."

Maria gathered the clothing and the dirty sheets, and followed Hanna a very short distance to the cove. As Maria scoped out her bathing area, Hanna said, "Hanna come back quick and bring you someting," and left. Maria found a good spot for soaking the clothes, where the freshwater spring carved a basin in the coral. She found a good flat rock to beat the clothes to get them clean.

When Hanna returned, she handed a small bottle of oil and two lemons to Maria, saying, "Dis fo' you to wash self. Da lemon berry good fo' hair, da oil good fo' yuh hurt body, rub gentle, and soon the hurt go away, Hanna know this."

Maria was struck by Hanna's tone and her kindness, and smiling broadly, Maria said, "Thank you, Hanna. Am I using up what is yours?"

"Oh no, Hanna no need."

While Maria finished her washing, Hanna hung the clothing on the surrounding branches and bushes. Later Maria cautiously stepped into the pool, while Hanna sat nearby like a sentinel keeping a protective watch over something valuable.

Questions and Answers

AFTER Maria finished bathing and washing her hair, Hanna helped her collect the clothes that were dry. As girls do when they work together, they talk. Maria, still feeling out of place, was full of why's. Why was she here? Her curiosity about the two women who helped her, why were they here? Where did they come from? Maria had question after question for Hanna.

Maria put on the chemise she found and washed. Of course, it was intended for someone quite a bit taller than she. She and Hanna had plaited several dry branches from the lohala palm they found near the tree and made several belts. Maria took one of the plaited pieces and tied it around her waist. At least she was covered now.

Hanna had gathered more dried leaves from the locale palm and a branch that had fallen. She wove the leaves together at one end, leaving the other end loose; then with a strong strip of hemplike leaf, she tied the woven part to the end of the branch she'd picked up. Smiling, she turned to Maria, "Yuh broom, Maria."

"Oh, Hanna, thank you, you are so helpful."

"Mama Henrietta teached me how to do tings, and she say, it the Bonin way. What you do fo' someone is good, and den dey he'p otha who need. Hanna have much ta tank Mama Henrietta. Now you have turn."

"Hanna, is Mama Henrietta your mother?"

"Oh no, Mama Henrietta jus' take me into her house when Mazarro bring me to Bonin."

"Mazarro brought you here! Oh, my goodness, when did you come here, and where did you come from? Were you stolen too?"

Hanna showed Maria the comb she brought with her.

"Let me comb yuh bootiful hair while you sit heah in sun, and den Hanna tell you story and maybe answer yuh question, okay?"

Combing Maria's beautiful hair in long strokes helped Hanna tell her story. Each stroke brought a new revelation, not only revealing but also relieving to both girls, a catharsis.

"My mama, my two sistahs, and me go beach near village…wait fo' fadda and uncles who go to sea fo' fish. We no bring food. Sistah run back to village. We look to sea and beeg boat with many mans come closer and closer to us. We scared…run away…but dese not good mans. Da pirates, dey catched us. Dey yellin' and screamin' words we not know. Da mans catch us and ties ropes round necks like animals, dey go to the village and capture otha womans, keel the old mans and leave childruns cryin' and screamin' for der mudders. Da pirates steel food and erthing dey could, then all da womans taked to pirate ship hidin' in da harbor. My old village in Ponape Island, da harbor is berry, berry beeg. When we get to pirate sheep, we put down to hold, weah dea more womans from odda islands. All of us 'fraid and cryin'. It ter'ble! Many womans not live on dis journey, many keeled or jus die. It berry bad, it take long time.

"After long time in hold and da sheep stop rockin' back forth, da sheep it slow down, we heah shoutin', we no unnerstan, but dis place, a berry busy place, many sheeps and many peopo. Here me mudder and sistah taken wid odda womans. A cheenaman, he wear long bootiful robe, big jewels, he pays pirate for womans, me mudda, me Sistah, and odda womans. Not me. I cry an' cry fo' me mudda, she and me sistah cry too, den dey gone.

"Nuddah man he take me, den he give me to dis old man. I berry, berry scared. Dis man not berry nice…he Mazarro. Berry bad man, he beat me, he do many bad tings…but like you, Maria, Hanna strong.

"Mazarro, he brings me to Bonin, den I meet Mama Henrietta, jus' lika I meet you, Maria. Mama Henrietta, she one good woman, she he'p me. Now you know 'bout Hanna's story, Maria."

Maria was speechless. *Does this happen everywhere? What can a girl do to help herself? Poor Hanna and all of us.*

"Hanna, did Mama Henrietta come to Bonin like we did?"

"One time Hanna ask Mama Henrietta, an' she say she come here wid five white mans, all speak funny. When she come, she is with small group of Sandwich Islanders, only five womans, the rest mans. The white mans bring us to help build a small village, the five wimmin to cook and maybe make babies for the white man. Mama Henrietta say it very hard first time here. Not like in Polynesia, only green trees, no flowers. She say it look berry sad.

"Soon the small groups from Polynesia build dea own village away from main harbor…here tings a litto different. Dey celebrate, dey play the ukulele an' drums. Dey sing story songs of dea old homes, dey make happy. Dey grow foods an ask ships dat come, to bring coconut trees an odda plants.

"Mama Henrietta, she her own woman, she no 'fraid nobody or any ting. She hav' one beeg heart too."

"Mama Henrietta is a good friend to have, isn't she?"

"Oh yeh, evr'body who know Mama Henrietta love her. All the sheep that come to Port Lloyd know 'bout her. She give bestes price for vegetables, fruit, da baskets she weaves, da meat…everting. She very beeg woman, beeger dan sum mans, but ever'body know her word berry good."

"It is good to hear your story, Hanna. Now I understand why you helped me, you said Mama Henrietta say it is the Bonin way, but it is also Mama Henrietta's way. She did for you what you did for me. How grateful I am for you and Mama Henrietta! How can I ever repay your kindnesses? Now it is time to get back to the cabin and finish my cleaning before Mazarro returns. Oh, and thank you for the broom, and your help too, Hanna."

"Maria, you goin' ta be all good? You want Hanna to help?"

"You don't have to, Hanna, you have helped me more than you know. I must face this situation on my own terms. You are a good friend."

Mazarro returned from the harbor in the afternoon, surprised to see that for some reason Maria had changed. Even the cabin smelled different.

I wonder what this is all about. Could be she is giving in. She's been a hard one to train. Full of surprises, she is. Hmmm!

Mazarro started toward her, but Maria turned abruptly and stared harshly at him. As small as she was, she stood straight and tall, hand on one hip, a look on her face that showed defiance, and in her other hand, she held on to the knife she was using. She was not going to allow him to intimidate or use her. Then she turned back to the chore at hand and continued cutting.

Taken aback, Mazarro stepped toward her anyway to stroke her hair, but Maria turned so quickly with the knife still in her hand that it threw him off guard.

"If you think that I am going to let you do what you want, you better think again," she uttered in a forbidding voice. "If you plan on my living here with you and sharing your bed, then you will not force me to do what you want. I will not allow you or anyone else to beat me or force me to be his slave. If you do, you will pay a high price. If you want peace, then it will be on my terms. No more are you going to hurt me!"

"Awright, awright, I give up!" Mazarro grudgingly answered, "jus' put the weapon down."

A WEEK after Maria expressed her demands, Mazarro, still treading lightly, returned from his duties at the harbor. Maria was not in sight.

"Maria, Maria!" he shouted. "Where are you?"

"I am here, just outside," she answered. "Why are you shouting?"

"What are you doing now?" he demanded.

Maria silently walked up to the shanty from the new garden she was planting. She knew that planting a garden this late might not be a wise move according to Mama Henrietta who was at her side.

Maria laughed when Hanna quipped, "Maybe Maria makes berry beeg change fo' herself. Maybe God make beeg change in weather fo' one mo' new garden, ya tink?"

Maria then turned to Mazarro and asked "What do you want, Mazarro?"

"I am leaving today on the *Portsmouth*, the island is in need of supplies," he shouted back.

"Are you sailing to Guam? If my family knows you are the one who stole me, you are a marked man. Maybe the *Portsmouth* will return without you. They may know who you are and where I am!" Maria harshly replied.

Mazarro said nothing, turned on his heel, picked up his sea bags, and left. He was ready to leave. He was no longer in control. The tables had changed.

After helping Maria clean up and set things in order, Hanna departed. Maria sat outdoors until the mosquitoes nearly made a meal out of her. She went in and prepared for a wonderful night away from the stress of the past weeks. Before falling asleep, she said a prayer of thanksgiving for this piece of good news.

Thank you, dear Father, for sending Mazarro away. Do my parents know who took me? Do they know where I am, Heavenly Father? If they know, why haven't they come for me?

She began to cry, feeling a deep loneliness for her family, and finally fell into a fitful sleep.

Maria was suddenly awakened by the sound of a large thunderclap that shook the little cabin. She jumped out of bed. Just as her feet touched the floor, another lightning bolt smashed into the ground, violently and close, with a deafening thunderclap leaving the air permeated with the smell of burned wood.

Frightened, Maria yanked a cover and threw it over her shoulders as she ran around, closing the doors and windows in this little shanty. Another lightning strike and then the inevitable thunderclap. *Where can I hide?*

As if on cue, the heavens opened, and the rain poured out. Shivering from the fear she was feeling, and from the cold air that surrounded her like a blanket, she thought, *This storm is big…a downpour and we're in the middle of it. The garden Hanna and I worked so hard on will be ruined.*

The rain seemed to last forever with winds making the rain sharp as needles. No one would be safe outdoors. Then Maria heard a sound, like someone or something banging at her door. *Who can be at my door?* As she turned to open the door, the wind almost took it out of her hands. She struggled to keep it from blowing off the hinges.

Standing against the strong wind was a drenched Millinchamp. Stunned, Maria motioned him to come in. He stood there soaked and uncomfortable, holding on to his hat, looking down, almost afraid to look Maria in the eye.

"Why are you here?" Maria shouted over the sounds of the wind and rain. A drenched and concerned Millinchamp responded, "Mazarro be sailing to the Sandwich Islands and is not due back for some months. This storm is a big one. Me thinks ye be safer on high ground, in the hills."

"Why do you think I need help from a storm? Storms don't bother me."

"'Tis not the storm, Maria, 'tis the warnin' blow. A dangerous typhoon be headin' right for Bonins. Ye must move up to high ground. Right away," he insisted.

"Why should I listen to your concerns over this storm? You were not concerned when that horrible Mazarro kept me prisoner! No, I do not need your help…now or ever! There are others who are nearby who have helped me. I can call on them. Thank you for the warning, but I do not need your help." She showed him to the door, shut and locked it. Now the rain came in torrents, and as it seeped from the roof, she found pots to collect it.

Her head whirled as she thought, *What nerve of him! Why, Joaquina and Millinchamp would be the last persons I would call on for help. I haven't given them a thought, even though I will never forget or forgive them for what they did. And now they wonder if I need help! What were they thinking? A typhoon! I'll take my chances.*

Lighting the whale-oil lamp, Maria looked for a piece of hardtack. She had been feeling queasy each day and thought she might be coming down with something. *The next time I see Mama Henrietta I will ask if she knows of an herb I could take for this queasy feeling.*

Maria crawled back into bed for warmth and a restless sleep.

The rain continued throughout the night, finally slowing to a gentle sprinkle at dawn. The day was turning out to be quite pretty. Just as fast as the rain came, it was gone. Maria began to dress and put things away.

There is something about rain that makes a person feel fresh and clean. Everything looks and smells fresh.

Looking out to the sea, she pondered, *The Sandwich Islands. Hmmm. So that's where Mazarro went…and away for several months. That's good news…life will be much easier, at least until he returns… very good news.*

The Typhoon

A LOUD knock at the door diverted Maria from her thoughts.
"Maria, Maria, come to door, is Hanna and Mama Henrietta."
Maria opened the door, happy to see them, but the look on their faces told her this was not a social visit.

Mama Henrietta excitedly announced, "No time visit. Beeg typhoon come, berry beeg! Hanna, have hardtack, fruit. Maria, take sum clothes, sum covers, and mantilla. We go up da hill to da caves…dey protect us. Come, hurry, wiki wiki! Ever'body go deah to be safe from typhoon. We go now!"

As the three began their trek up the mountain, Maria could make out others ahead of them. It seemed that everyone was scattered around the paths as they climbed up to the caves away from the impending storm. Even the wild goats were heading up to the top of the mountain, their white heads bobbing as they moved through the brush. There was no sound from the islanders except the shuffling of feet as they scurried up the hill.

Maria wondered, *where is this storm. Why is everyone so anxious? No wind! The sun is shining, there are some dark clouds, but they seem to be far off to the south of us. I have experienced many typhoons on Guam. None of them were like this one. Oh well, it is better to follow the people who know what to do.*

After they had been climbing for what seemed a long time, snaking in and out of the trees and brush, the caves came into view. Soon everyone would be able to breathe a sigh of relief.

Before the three women entered the cave and its relative safety, the winds began to pick up, but soon the sun hid from view, and the winds, ever stronger, made it harder to move ahead in the last short distance.

Mama Henrietta shouted, "Keep head down, beeg rain come before we get deah."

The air became heavier, and the rain began, first in small gentle drops, hardly noticeable. Just as they entered the mouth of this enormous cave, the wind blew so hard, the trees were laid flat. Some of the islanders held on to each other for support. It rained harder than anyone could remember…sharp sheets of rain felt like hot steel as it pelted the body. The last of the islanders made it to the cave just before the main part of the typhoon hit their shores.

"Ah, now we be safe til da storm pass!" Mama Henrietta shouted over the sound of the storm.

The wind now at full force, whistled through the crevasses of the volcanic rock, toppling trees, flattening undergrowth and structures. No man could withstand its fury.

Suddenly it turned colder. The mouth of the cave was wide, but as one moved farther into the cave for protection, it became quite dark. Ship's lanterns were lighted. The cave was large enough for all the islanders to settle in with a reasonable degree of comfort for the duration of the storm. Without the lanterns' light, the cave would be pitch-black deeper into its belly.

Maria, shivering from the dash up to the cave and the cold dampness, was glad for the mantilla she wrapped over her shoulders. She was a stranger to everyone but Millinchamp, Joaquina, Mama Henrietta, and Hanna. *There are many people here, and they all seem to know what to do*, Maria observed. *Mama Henrietta is busy making sure everyone is taken care of. Everyone smiles when they see her.*

Hanna helped store the supplies with some of the men from the village. When she finished her task, she sat down next to Maria. "Dis typhoon berry beeg, maybe two or t'ree day, den we go home, all finished."

"How do you know?" Maria asked.

"Mans from Bonin an' womans too, dey know da sea, dey read sign in da sky, feel da weather in deah body. Dey tells Mama, but she awready know dat. Ever'body listen when dey say beeg storm com, den ever'body work togetter afta storm go."

Maria asked, "What can I do to help, Hanna?"

"We ask Mama Henrietta, pretty soon need much he'p."

As they settled for the duration of the storm, someone started a fire; someone else began playing a ukulele. The music seemed to calm everyone, especially the children. Some women gathered to plait baskets, gossip, and carry on as they would at home. As the typhoon reached its full force, the rains and the winds were incessant, not letting up. Some of the men worked at the mouth of the cave trying to keep the water from rushing in.

Mama Henrietta was speaking with a man, a person who seemed to have authority over the others.

"Who is that man, Hanna?" Maria asked curiously.

"Him?" Hanna asked as she looked toward the man Maria pointed out with a motion of her head.

"Oh, heem, dat Mistah Savory; he da governor heah. He berry respect man by all da peopo dat liv heah. He talk to Mama all time. She keep heem up on all news on island. You wanna meet heem?"

"Oh no, not now, everybody is busy, maybe another time," Maria answered.

Maria Meets Savory

T HE island was devastated by the typhoon, most of the dwellings flattened or blown out to sea. Pieces of the destruction could be seen washing back and forth against the rocky shore before being taken out with the tide.

Work parties were assembled to begin salvaging anything they could find. Each team was given certain areas to clean up and restore, just enough so the resident would have a dry place to live in temporarily.

The canoes that were stored safely from this storm were pulled from their hiding places and put in the water to find and salvage anything usable floating in the harbor, a seemingly insurmountable task. Yet the spirit of the Bonin people made the rebuilding a cheerful job. Everyone who could pitched in the Bonin way.

Maria's body was finally healing from the last Mazarro encounter. Now able to assist with the cleanup as a member of Hanna's team, she and the three other women worked steadily for several hours, moving tree branches to a designated place where they will later be salvaged, clearing the area where a house stood. Then the team would be able to gather any household and personnel items for later identification by the people who resided there.

"Hanna, have you found anything we can save?" Maria asked.

"Here, Hanna fin' someting in dat bush, don't know wat dis is?"

Maria went to see what Hanna found. Quietly looking down at the item, she fell to her knees, recognizing the item as a camisole she'd embroidered for Joaquina's sixteenth birthday. Shaken by the discovery, Maria gently pulled and unraveled the camisole from the bush, and began to cry quietly.

Hanna was puzzled with her reaction, not knowing what to make of it. She patted Maria's shoulder very gently and cooed, "Is all right to cry, Maria, is all right. Sum tings too hard to unnerstan… we all feel sorry."

Maria took a deep breath and answered, "Oh, Hanna, I made this camisole for my Aunt Joaquina. This is hers."

"Maria, dat is good news, maybe we find more stuff. Den we find Millinchamp and give him da news. Dis place Millinchamp's. He have new woman now…maybe she your auntie."

Brushing aside the comment about her aunt, Maria said, "We'll keep cleaning up the debris, Hanna. This house will be the next one to be rebuilt, according to Mama Henrietta. When we find more of their things, we will set them aside in a neat pile."

"Dis woman of Millinchamp, is she you' aunt, Maria? Why you not answer me?"

"I can't right now, Hanna, but I promise to explain later. It is too hard for me to talk about this to anyone, especially now. We need to keep working, so why don't we go through the area as fast as we can."

Hanna gave Maria a look dat said *Hanna no give up fo' answer, Maria.* Then she went about gathering things from the hiding places the winds and rains had made. The girls found quite a few items, even a large sea trunk that made it through the typhoon without a scratch.

After they finished going over the Millinchamp property, Hanna said, "I berry hungry, you too, Maria?"

Out came a package from Hanna's skirt pocket. She called the other two women, "Come, we eat now."

The two women also had some food to share, so all four pooled their food. While eating, Hanna introduced Maria to Celia and Tomasina, two of the original twenty-five Sandwich Islanders who came with Mama Henrietta. They chatted like women often do when they share food.

After they ate, the four women finished their cleanup and proceeded to their next place, passing where Mazarro's shanty once stood and where Maria lived. There was a team in the process of cleaning up there. They continued down to the village where Hanna and Mama Henrietta lived.

"Hanna, aren't we going to work here?" Maria asked. "No, we go to other house. Other crew work here and at da village. Ever'body have dea job, we know be for typhoon hit."

Maria nodded her head in agreement, and they moved on down past the village and Mazarro's place. The Mazarro shanty, where Maria lived, was totally blown away; the Polynesian village below the shanty was flattened, as it sat right on the shoreline. It seemed that nothing survived.

Having learned from the past, typhoons were not new to the natives. In their farsightedness, food was stored in caves up on the mountain, along with some building materials and other essential supplies. So even though the island was nearly destroyed, the islanders would survive.

The old-timers knew how to read a storm, approximately how big, and the timing of its arrival. This was almost second nature to them. The fishermen could tell by the way the fish reacted, by the feeling the sea gave them. They knew. They acted on nature's clues regarding the weather.

Looking around, Maria noticed how many trees had been destroyed, wondering, *How can we rebuild? So many houses are gone, nothing standing, the trees, especially the cabbage palm…I don't see any at all. What will the men use for roofs?*

As if Hanna could read Maria's mind, she said, "Two canoes sail to odda side of island…maybe dey come back with fresh cabbage palm leaves. Den we make new roofs for new houses. Pritty soon evating look good."

Lean-tos were set up at the sight of their former dwellings for temporary protection from the elements. Outhouses were built over their original sites. The organizers took great care in seeing to the health of their people. Mr. Savory knew how to organize and make things happen. Yet it was still a daunting task, one the islanders experienced quite frequently during the typhoon months from June to December.

Freshwater was the one resource this island had plenty of along with the islander's spunk and the will to carry on. With no doctor on the island, the people were left to use remedies they learned from the past, and many of the herbs had been picked and stored in protected places. The governor kept a watchful eye over any medical outbreak. He had a few islanders assisting him in this area, like Mama Henrietta.

Maria slowly worked her way through a pile of rubble that had once been someone's home. Hanna worked her way around the area trying to clear a spot for the men to rebuild. She looked up at Maria and saw her stagger a little then right herself.

"Maria, you okay?"

"Just got up too fast," she responded. "I better get some water, it is getting very warm out here. It would be nice to bathe though. Where are we, right now?"

"Oh, dis is Mistah Savory's teahouse. He live here in dah back," Hanna answered. "We almos' finish…keep lookin' for tings not broke. Look, dis bottle not scratch, what it say, Maria?"

Maria read the label. "It says Royal Guard fine whiskey, brewed in England. Look there are more untouched bottles: rum from

Cuba…where is that? King Edward, Royal blend scotch. Look over there, beer bottles, lots of them. Are you sure this is a teahouse, Hanna?"

"Oh yes, Mistah Savory maybe use dese bottles for sick peopo, you tink? We ask when we see heem. Maybe we find safe place to keep the medicine and tell Mistah Savory. Okay, Maria?"

"It's certainly all right with me, but did we find any tea boxes? We better look, and when we finish here, we need to check on the village, then go to the shanty…maybe we'll be able to start putting things back in its place."

"Maybe," Hanna responded.

The sun was high in the sky, and things were progressing as fast as they could. Out in the harbor, the ships were beginning to sail back into port. They all left for the high seas before the typhoon hit. The return was a good sign. These ships brought more manpower and much needed supplies.

Mr. Savory rounded the bend and walked toward his old tea house, or where it had stood. He noticed two women cleaning up the debris. He knew Hanna, but this was the first time he'd seen the young woman Mazarro had spirited away from.

Hanna spotted him and ran over to give him a hug, saying, "Mistah Savory, we work your house now, hope we find many tings for you. Maria, Maria, come ova. Mistah Savory, he is heah."

She is a beauty even as dirty as she is, Savory thought, *I wonder how she is getting along. Mama Henrietta has been telling me about her and how badly she has been treated. That Mazarro, he's been a bad one from the start.*

"Ah, Senorita"—bowing his head toward Maria—"Mama Henrietta has been telling me about you. As chief magistrate of Bonin, I offer you my sincere apologies for the actions of one of our citizens, and I will see to it that the men of the village rebuild your place right away."

Looking around his property, he thanked them for all their efforts.

Maria smiled broadly and replied, "Mazarro is not here, Mr. Savory. I do hope he didn't survive the typhoon, and I say that truthfully. Thank you for your apology, but it means nothing at the moment." Maria turned to leave, and she looked back at Savory and said, "So this place of yours is called a teahouse? We didn't find tea, however we found a lot of liquor." Smiling, she continued, "The salts comin' back to shore will be very sick and will be needing their tea! We put the tea in a safe place. It was nice to meet you, Mr. Savory."

Savory stood feet apart, hands on his hips, and let out an enormous laugh, as he nodded good-bye and thought, *This little girl's got spunk. Certainly ain't shy. This little senorita is probably more of a handful than Mr. Mazarro bargained for. Good for her.*

"Well, Ms. Maria Del Los Santos y Castro, you have a sense of humor. I named my place *Savory's Teahouse* just for fun, and never fooled a soul until now. Hahaha! Thank you for cheering me up. Good day to you." *Now I understand why Mazarro took to the sea. She may be young, but she is feisty.*

Mama Henrietta Consoles Maria

A MONTH after the typhoon devastated the island, the small population moved back into their rebuilt homes, with scattered livestock, chickens, geese, ducks, and other fowl recaptured. Vegetable gardens once again started, making life return to a somewhat normal stage.

Maria was pleased to have a better house to live in now: two rooms, an outdoor kitchen, and an outhouse located close by. She kept the house and surrounding grounds spotless even though a huge dark cloud loomed over her. She was carrying Mazarro's child, a terrible blow to her, and he was expected to return within a few weeks.

She asked herself, *Why is this happening? That horrible man, he steals me from my parents and the only home I ever knew, he beats me, rapes me, impregnates me. I don't know anything about having babies. Mama Henrietta told me I am maybe three to four months pregnant, maybe less, but this child could be borne by the end of the year, maybe sooner…I don't know. I wonder what Mazarro will do when he finds out? He is a miserable excuse of a man!*

Horrified and ashamed, Maria turned to Mama Henrietta for solace. Still a naive fifteen-year-old, she needed the comforting ways of a mother. Mama Henrietta filled that need. Longing for her mother's arms, Maria snuggled deeper into Mama Henrietta's arms sobbing and sobbing.

Through her panting breath, Maria uttered, "Oh, Mama, how much I miss my own mama…I need her so much! Mazarro…I will never get away from him. He took me against my wishes, and Joaquina let him, and now I am pregnant. Oh, Mama Henrietta, what can I do? I have no money, this house is not even mine, Mama, please help me. I am so scared!"

She sobbed so hard, her body shook. Mama Henrietta, holding Maria as she tried to calm her, cooed, "Is awright, baby girl, you' be fine, we take care for you. Maria, you have choice! You no need have baby!"

Maria, her face contorted from crying so hard, looked at Mama Henrietta in shock and said, "I can't do that, Mama, I can't do that…no, I won't do that…and how could you even say I'd do something like that? No matter how bad things can be, I will not kill this baby."

"Dat's a good choice, Maria. Now Mama know wat you want, an' I will be deah to hep every day. You know Mama no hurt you evr'. You make good choice! Now we git to work, make you strong fo' babee, and you be fine. Oh, 'bout Mazarro, I be told he git tru da typhoon. He know how ta do dat. He good sailor, but dat all he good fo'. He come back maybe one month, maybe two month more. You be plenny big wid babee by den."

So, he is safe. God doesn't seem to hear my prayers, Maria thought. *One good thing, he won't be returning soon.*

The new, larger cabin built to replace the little shanty gave Maria a sense of belonging, even though it wasn't hers, but that didn't matter. She set about making it livable as though the house belonged to her, at least until Mazarro returned.

Hanna and Maria began preparing their garden, making sure there were sweet potatoes, taro, pumpkin, string beans, and other vegetables they could sell to the visiting whalers. Both of the girls, with Mama's suggestions, spent a great deal of time working out a watering system. It took some doing, but to their surprise, it was a success and the talk of the village. Mama Henrietta was responsible for the talk, thinking, *I have bragging rights.*

Maria and Hannah shared the work in their bountiful garden and their income. Maria, after paying her share of the supplies, put her earnings in a safe place. Having nothing when Mazarro stole her, not even enough clothing to cover her body, her immediate needs would now be taken care of. She was becoming a clever businesswoman.

Patting Maria on the belly, Mama Henrietta lovingly said, "Ever'body happy you with babee. Dey say you be good mudder. Ever'body makin' sumting berry speshol fo' babee. Mama happy too, but I not happy wid Mazarro. He is a berry bad man, berry bad,"

"I have been feeling so ashamed," Maria replied. "Oh, Mama Henrietta, thank you for sharing this news with me. I am so happy you are here."

"You not be shamed, no, no, no. You jus' li'l girl, you not know how bad man is. Dars many bad peopo eva place. Me too have same ting like you an nobody he'p. You, me, all da girls, we tink good tauts, not bad tauts 'n' we make tings right fo' all us. Maria, we stick togedder, we he'p you with babee, okay? You know, dis Bonin good place cause we have Mistah Savory. He da bestes fo' us. Someday you know too, Maria."

Joaquina Extends Her Hand In Peace

Aᖴᴛᴇʀ Hanna told Henrietta about her suspicions of Maria's pregnancy, Mama questioned Maria and calculated that Maria was with child. Maria did not take the news well. She was horrified, humiliated that this child was Mazarro's, the man she hated.

Mama had projected that Maria was about three or four months along, maybe even a little more, but she was definitely expecting. As Maria's baby grew within her, she, Hanna, and Mama Henrietta prepared for its arrival. Mazarro hadn't yet returned from his travels, but Maria heard he would arrive within the month. Quite independent by this time, Maria didn't look forward to that day.

Maria wondered, *what will Mazarro do when he returns? If he didn't know of my pregnancy, how would he? Furthermore, how would he react? It has been a long time, and I have been very much on my own. I must prepare for whatever comes.* She did not look forward to his return.

Maria and Hanna were busy harvesting the corn they had grown, chatting up a storm as close friends often did. Maria caught a movement out of the corner of her eye and quickly looked up. Standing at the edge of the row they were harvesting was Millinchamp. *Oh no, what does he want?* Maria pondered.

Hanna turned to look, and seeing Millinchamp, she jumped up and ran toward him. Smiling at Hanna, Millinchamp prepared for her boisterous hello. Throwing her arms around his neck, she said excitedly, "Mistah Millinchamp, nice ta see you, you come to see garden, berry big one, yes?"

"Aye, 'tis a big garden," Millinchamp responded, "but I am here to give a message to Maria."

"What kind of message would you have for me?" Maria asked.

"The cap'n of the *Pearl* docked today, had a message for Savory regarding Mazarro's arrival. I thought you betta know…he sails into Port Lloyd in four days. Oh, and your aunt Joaquina sends her love."

"So Mazarro will return in four days. Thank you," Maria responded as she clumsily got up from where she sat, turned, and slowly wobbled haughtily back to the cabin, saying nothing more.

Millinchamp had prepared for her curt response. Even so, he seemed taken aback by Maria's reaction. Now that she was large with child, he had concerns for her. No one knew Mazarro like he and Savory knew him. Both believed the devil himself lived within his heart. Millinchamp decided to go to Savory for help. *It's obvious Maria won't take my advice. Maybe Savory can help. If anyone can, he would be the one.*

John Millinchamp returned to his Joaquina and their shanty disappointed. He knew that Joaquina awaited his return and hoped upon hope that Maria had softened over the past months. Joaquina missed her niece so much and was sad, desperate to be forgiven for her selfishness. She had urged John to go and warn Maria of Mazarro's return.

Trying to stay calm, Joaquina grabbed a broom and went outside to tidy up. She nervously walked back and forth in their yard, watching for John to return from Maria's.

As he walked slowly into the yard, he knew she was anxiously waiting for some sign that all was well between her and Maria. John was disappointed…she could see it in his face. *Oh, this didn't go well. He looks defeated. Aye, dios mio, he looks like he lost his last friend. What could have happened?*

Dropping the broom, she ran toward him, shouting, "John! John! What happened? Are you all right? What did Maria say to you? Oh, John, I am so sorry."

Millinchamp held Joaquina as he uttered, "She's an unforgiving girl, Joaquina, she might as well have stabbed me in me heart. Unforgiving she is. Don't know what Mazarro is like, he be gone near seven months or so. What's to tell how a man will be, after so long? He has not been good to any woman of his, notta one. He even killed a girl fo' not doin' his biddin'. He's no good, Joaquina. I shoulda known better…if anything happens to her, it will surely be on my conscience."

Joaquina began to cry. "No, John, I was the one, blinded by my love for you. I was only thinking of my happiness, not anyone else's."

John continued, "She is big with this baby. Hard ta tell how Mazarro will act when he sees her. Best I report my feelin' to Nathaniel so he can keep an eye on the girl. I know Henrietta keeps him informed. She and Hanna have adopted Maria since we arrived. At least, Maria is in good hands."

"My niece should have been safe with me," Joaquina wailed. "Instead, my action put her in harm's way. Why was I so foolish? Why didn't you tell me about Mazarro and his cruelty? Did you think Mazarro had changed his ways?"

"I know, I know, my love, you cannot blame yourself. When I captained the ship, I was in charge of everyone's welfare on board. Instead I chose to ignore even the complaints of my men. You are not responsible, I am. Your niece was in great danger, and I chose to ignore it, even though the reputation of Mazarro and his cruelty is widely known. God only knows what is in store for Maria when he returns, but she has proven to be a very industrious and capable young woman. For that I thank the good Lord."

Millinchamp walked over to Savory's Teahouse later that afternoon and expressed his concerns about Mazarro's return, saying, "As a member of this community and a longtime friend, I have come to ask you for help regarding the little girl, Maria, the one Mazarro stole from the island of Guam.

"I reported his actions toward the girl while on board the *Portsmouth* after we arrived in Port Lloyd. We both know his reputation with wimmin especially. My concern now is Maria's pregnancy. She is large with child and may not be able to protect herself from his bad moods. Maria's aunt, Joaquina, is my wife, you know that Maria holds hard feelings against both of us.

"She will not accept any help except from Mama Henrietta and Hanna. They have been her angels. I know how violent Mazarro can be, and during that voyage, I chose to overlook what could have been avoided, which I reported upon our return. Now my conscience is driving me mad, and I need to do something. Will you help me, Nate?"

Savory replied, "As magistrate of this island, I watch over the welfare of the people. As a longtime friend, ye can be sure of my help. Henrietta, one of our oldest friends, has kept me aware of the little Chamorro girl. Don't worry, John, I will help as much as I can. We have both known Matteo Mazarro a very long time. Now, how about sharing a bottle of tea with me?"

Maria's Strength Emerges

M ARIA heard Mazarro's voice before she saw him enter the property. She and Hanna had been shucking corn to prepare it for grinding. Hanna looked up first as Mazarro came in carrying his sea bag.

Maria barely recognized his voice. It did not sound like the person who left almost nine months ago. She felt a shudder go through her body; a feeling of dread went through her. She shook off the feeling and thought, *I have more to be concerned about right at the moment. So now he is back. Is he less cruel, less hateful? I know what he is capable of doing. Now I have more at stake. God, please protect the baby and give me strength.*

Mazarro knew through the grapevine, so to speak, that Maria was pregnant. He had no idea how far along, nor did he care. He didn't expect to find her quite like this. Shocked to see her so large, he blurted out, "What the hell is this? Ye been knocked up. Whose kid ye carryin'?" Yet he knew. He knew.

Maria looked at him in disgust. "You son of Satan, who do you think did this to me? No more will you treat me with disrespect. No more will you lord it over me, Mr. Mazarro," she spat out. "I am not afraid of you or anyone else."

Mazarro shrugged, rolled his eyes, and said no more.

Maria went into labor a little over two weeks later. With the help of both his new aunties, Hanna and Mama Henrietta, he came into the world screaming his little head off, a healthy boy she named John.

Mama Henrietta stayed with Maria, teaching her what to do.

When Maria's milk came, Henrietta showed Maria little tricks to keep Johnny awake long enough to fill his belly. Mama Henrietta noticed that Mazarro lingered on the outskirts of the cabin and thought, *He up to sumting, maybe good, maybe bad…betta find out.*

She gave instructions to Hanna, "You be heah fo' Maria. She not do anyting fo' maybe ten days, so fix all da food…make sure she git plenny wata, plenny food…no give Maria food ta make babee an' Maria sick, okay? You need coconut milk wid breadfruit, plenny fish, plenny egg, an' gets milk now so babee have good food."

For the ten days, Maria remained in bed. Hanna took care of all their needs. She prepared all the food and other chores Maria could not do. Mama Henrietta went out to check on Mazarro and found him at the lean-to. She noticed how thin he became and how gray his hair had turned. This didn't deter her mission; she was not afraid of any man and scurried right up to him. Her hands on her hips and feet slightly apart, she gave Mazarro a real talking-to about his boy.

She scolded him for ignoring his son, saying, "When man have son, dey berry proud, dey happy fo' dat. You, Matteo, you not happy for what you make. Dis babee is betta fo' his mudder…she make heem berry proud of his line, you see. Now you go see your son, he berry nice babee, berry nice. Maria do good work. And no mo' you hurt Maria or da babee, you unnerstan, Mazarro? I be watchin' you fo' sure!

Mazarro listened to Mama Henrietta and, as she turned to leave, said, "Gracias, but I do not belong here. I don't know about these things."

Mama Henrietta turned and said, "What you spec when you do chi chi wit wimmin? Aye, you unnerstan! Dis girl, she good girl, you betta treat her an' babee good, you heah me?" Then she left him to think.

Hanna had just changed and washed Johnny and cooed an old song she remembered from so many years ago. She looked up and saw Mazarro standing in the entry. Maria had fallen asleep, and Hanna motioned for Mazarro to enter. As he entered, she put her finger to her lips and *shhhed* to let him know not to waken Maria. The baby stirred in Hanna's arms, kicked, and looked up with wide-open eyes, taking everything in. Mazarro, intrigued by this little being, moved closer to get a better look at his son. Hanna shoved Johnny into his father's arms and stepped away.

For a little while, the two, father and son, stared at each other. Mazarro softened and could not get over the fact that this was his child. *How can this be? How can this small packet be from me? Will he grow up to be a good man, or will he be like me? I know, little boy, you cannot be like your father, you must do better.* He returned the baby to Hanna, who placed him near his mother.

Mazarro left with a bottle of rum, climbed up into the hills surrounding the village, and entered one of the caves. He needed to be alone. He had few friends, and most knew this man had many dark days, especially when he drank. Mazarro had much on his mind. While in Shanghai, a Chinese herb doctor warned him that his constant cough seemed to worsen. He prescribed herbs to help him and then warned him, "No drink." Mazarro didn't heed the advice. He went about his daily habit of drinking, fighting, and carousing.

Here I am, a man of over sixty, a father for the first time. How long will my life last? Will I see the boy grow up? Maria, she hates the sight of me, I don't blame her. I never had no one like her, so beautiful, so young. She has the strength of a caribou. I have been cruel, I know. I am getting too old to sail more than one or two times. I'll try to do better, but…who knows. The people here, especially Henrietta and Savory, will gut me and feed me to the sharks if I hurt Maria again. And nobody will care one bit. I should have a drink but no more for me. It makes a man crazy, and I don't want to push my luck.

Mazarro poured the bottle of rum onto the ground and returned to the lean-to near the cabin.

Mazarro Legacy

Almost a month later, Mazarro moved from the lean-to back into the cabin. He and Maria had a quiet, uncomfortable peace. Life went on. The boy brought him some joy. Johnny smiled a lot and loved it when his mother would sing her songs from Guam. Hanna and Mama Henrietta stayed close, and the three women made sure the baby grew stronger and protected.

Mazarro tried hard to be gentler and managed to get Maria to allow him to return to her bed, and when Johnny was almost four months old, she found herself pregnant once more and was horrified.

Becoming very distraught, her milk slowed down, and Johnny cried for more and more. He was not getting enough nourishment, and finally Mama Henrietta said, "Maria, you carry 'nother babee… means you not have milk fo' Johnny boy, he need mo' and mo'. Two tings we do. We give heem banana leetle bit, den we give heem jus' a leetle bit wid honey an' leetle milk, den we git other woman who have much milk to he'p heem, you unnerstan, Maria?

"Mama git you woman who have much milk, Johnny Boy need milk to grow strong. You no worry, Johnny Boy awready know his own mama, you see."

In the daytime, Johnny stayed with his mother. His wet nurse, with her own child, stayed with them. At night, he went to the wet nurse's house. As Mama said, "Evating goin' ta be awright."

Maria's second pregnancy, different from her first, seemed to go along well. Mazarro went out to sea for short trips, as a change had come over him. He wanted to be close by when the second baby arrived. He returned from his second voyage greeted with the news that Maria was once more in labor and soon to deliver. He was almost sixty-two years old and very ill with syphilis.

Baby Arita was born, a bright-eyed little girl weighing in at three kilos, smaller than her brother. Johnny was just over one-year old and beginning to walk. And oh, how he could jabber. Once again Hanna and Mama Henrietta were there to help.

Besides himself, Mazarro didn't know how he could be so fortunate as to have a boy and a girl. Maria took charge of the children. She made sure Johnny knew his father. She had vowed that her son would never be like Mazarro, but he needed to know him.

On a trail leading to the caves, three months after Arita was born, Nathaniel found Mazarro beaten beyond recognition but still alive. Savory called for help, and two men from the village carried him to his cabin. Mazarro soon died from his wounds and his disease.

Maria became a very young widow, with two babies. Mazarro had earlier scribbled out a will generously leaving her the property and what money he had. Maria did not mourn Mazarro. That part of her life was over. She quietly prayed a prayer of thanksgiving. Maria knew her life would be different. The load was lifted off her young shoulders. She thanked God for her good fortune. Although alone again, she wasn't lonely. She had Mama Henrietta, Hanna, and many friends to see her through this period.

True to his word to Mama Henrietta and John Millinchamp, Nathaniel Savory stepped forward and helped Maria make sense of Mazarro's personal estate. This helped to deepen the friendship between the two, the New Englander and the kidnapped girl.

Mama Henrietta watched as their friendship grew. *Ah, now dis berry good sign. See, God, you take long time for dis. Why you not see befo'?*

Maria's Life Changes

MARIA'S life evidenced much change for the better after Mazarro's death. The two children, Johnny and Arita, thrived under the watchful eyes of their mother and the aunties. Johnny Boy, a very energetic twenty-one-month-old boy, never slowed down and had the energy of a hundred-knot gale. This little boy had a curious nature. He was into everything, a handful on his own. The two babies brought great joy to Maria. Playing with Johnny Boy brought her pleasure as he had a hearty and infectious laugh.

Carrying baby Arita on her back while she did chores, Maria sang and talked to her. When Maria bathed and changed Baby Girl, the little one's eyes would follow her mother's movement, and looking into her mother's eyes, she wondered, *Who are you, pretty lady? Your voice is like an angel's when you sing.*

Maria loved this little girl, thinking, *Boys are very different from girls. Johnny is like the winds of a northern storm, blowing every which way, trying to show its power. Arita is a calm breeze, moving about softly kissing the trees. There is such a difference.*

Arita, at nine months, still hadn't tried to crawl, stand, or walk. Some babies her age did all these things, even walked. *Not my Baby Girl, she is content being held, had little appetite, never fussed, and could sleep forever it seemed.*

Something about this little girl drew Mama to her. She sensed that Arita wasn't right. She was slow to grasp things and seldom cried. Arita sometimes had a blank stare when she looked at anyone. Yet when tickled she giggled.

Mama thought, *Maybe Mama too quick to find sumting wrong, God know what he doin', but Mama no can stop worry.*

True to his words to Millinchamp and Mama Henrietta, Savory visited the Mazarro family. He often visited all the areas and some of the inhabitants to see how things were going, yet he took a special liking to this young girl still in her teens. *She is one tough girl, no doubt about it, and she is smart. Have to admit, Matteo got his self someone smarter than him. May he rest in peace, though he does not deserve it.*

Mama Henrietta stayed close by whenever Nathaniel Savory came to visit. After the first two visits, she wondered, *Wat he wait fo', nobody heah to stop heem. He go too slow, he wait fo' maybe a typhoon or sumting? Maria, she like heem too. Savory he not young no mo', he betta know life not wait long.*

While Henrietta worried about Nathaniel and his slow action toward Maria, she never thought that Maria could have feelings for him too. Maria didn't indicate one thing, never asked where he could be, did he have a woman, none of the questions one might ask if they had strong feelings. Even Nathaniel couldn't be sure, but the two of them would flirt with each other like two teenagers. All Maria knew was when Nathaniel didn't come by the cabin, she wondered where he was and what he was doing.

Nathaniel Savory's visits became the talk of the island. His current woman heard the scuttlebutt and flew into a rage, and he didn't deny the friendship. He responded in exasperation, "I just enjoy the conversations I have with Maria. It really isn't quite what it seems. We are nevah alone, Mama Henrietta and Hanna are always there."

A few days later, Maria heard a booming sound coming from Yankeetown just over the hill. Suddenly Hanna appeared and shouted, "Come, come, Maria, take Arita, I take Johnny Boy, I have food an' wata, Come quick, we hafta hide, bad mens tear up everting in Yankeetown…try to keel evr'body! Dey has guns! Dey steels all da animals, shoot da peopo. Many not die, but I don' know, Mama not come back so you an' me an' babees we hide."

Stunned, Maria grabbed her children and a few things and moved quickly into the hills, following the ocean as a guide but far enough off not to be noticed. Hanna carried Johnny on her back. Maria carried Arita in a large scarf in which she used to lay Baby Girl. She drew the four corners up and tied them to the back of her neck, so the baby in a womblike condition could feel her mother's heartbeat and be calmed. Arita fell asleep with the movement as they hurried to safety.

Luckily, the warm weather continued as the little band left with very few things to protect them. The sound of screams and shooting could still be heard in the distance as they continued moving away from harm. The two babies were quiet. Johnny Boy found this to be great fun. He could ride Hanna like she was a horse. He kept singing, "Giddyap, giddyap! Whoopee!"

Dis is good, Hanna thought.

The girls arrived at their safe place, far enough away that no one could find or hear them. Hanna, seeing smoke coming from her village and smoke coming from Yankeetown, thought, *I hope we not stay here too long, we have on'y food fo' two days.*

They took turns standing watch throughout the day and night. The children slept well, and Johnny Boy explored the area, Maria making sure he didn't wander too far away as he wanted to do. The next day, no more screaming or hollering…even the smoke they had seen earlier had died down.

"Maria, me tink evating all finish. Doz pirates dey gone. Now maybe we go home. Wat you tink?"

"Let's wait, what if they are still there and just resting or moving the loot onto their ships to start stealing again? What would we do then?" Maria asked.

"Maybe you right, Maria, we have 'nuff food fo' one more day. We stay. I be berry sad if anyting happen our babies. I wonder if Mama okay."

"Me too, Hanna."

Nathaniel's Thoughts of Maria

T HE Bonin Islanders were devastated by the attack from the men of the *Saint Andrew* and the *Maid of Australia*. Savory, an old salt himself, was openly angered by the assault. He wanted to react, to fight in kind, but the outnumbered islanders had only a few guns and ammunition. Their only other source of weapons were the knives and machetes used for daily survival.

Savory's only way to respond to the attack was to do nothing, so he controlled his feelings. He knew that his actions would set the tone for the islanders to get over the dirty deeds of those men as life had to go on for the community, and it did. Nathaniel would not forget the attack and felt one day the crews of the two vessels would receive their due. And so, they did.

John Millinchamp stopped by the teahouse for a chat. Nathaniel thought, *The old boy looks totally defeated, poor salt*, and said, "Good to see you, John, what do I owe this visit from you, my friend?"

"Nate, it has been damn frustrating trying to do everything over and over. If it's not a typhoon, it's some crazy sailors taking everything we work for away. Poor Joaquina! She longs for a connection with her niece, Maria, ignoring the fact that her aunt lives here, won't have anything to do with her. Joaquina misses her family, and she's pregnant…very emotional, so me thinks we best try to go back to Guam as soon as possible. Can ye help us?"

Nathaniel wasn't surprised with the news. He well knew about the rift between Joaquina and Maria. He was aware that Joaquina did not quite fit in with the others. He knew that were it not for Joaquina's selfishness, Maria would not be in Bonin. He also knew through Henrietta's reports how Maria blamed both of the Millinchamps for the way Mazarro treated her. So, he understood the position John was in. He commiserated with John and agreed that on the *Portsmouth*'s next trip they would be aboard.

"Why, John, have you waited so long to leave?" Nathaniel went on. "Didcha give it a thought maybe nothin' would change between these ladies?"

"I just thought with time, maybe, it would," Millinchamp said sadly. "But nothing we did would soften that little girl's heart. Maria was right, Joaquina and me shoulda stood up for her, and we didn't. We only thought of ourselves. We did her no favors, no sir. We will rest in hell, I just know it."

Nate grinned and said, "The *Portsmouth* will be sailing for Guam in ten days. Will this give you enough time to getcher things together? Otherwise, it will be two months or so." As he poured rum into two cups, he added, "You an' me, we been together a long time, I know you and Mazarro hated me guts, but that's water under the bridge, John. Here's to your future!"

John responded, "Out of the five original settlers on the Bonin, two have died and one returned to the Sandwich Islands. We are the last two, an' soon it will only be you, Nate."

They drank their cups of rum, shook hands, and parted.

Joaquina anxiously awaited John's return to hear Savory's response. She sat rocking back and forth on the porch cocking her ears for any sound of him. She heard someone whistling a sea shanty. *Is that John? I've never heard him whistle before.*

Millinchamp rounded the corner of the porch and answered her unspoken question with a big smile on his face. "Start a packin', me love, we leave in ten days on the *Portsmouth*. Tell that little one yer carryin 'tis Guam he'll be born on, just like his ma."

"Thank you, John, thank you!" Joaquina said with joy. "I dearly miss my family."

A short time after Millinchamp had left Nathaniel, Mama Henrietta stopped by the teahouse with some vegetables from one of the gardens. She saw Nate out on the back porch, so she headed around the corner. "Whatcha up to, Nate?"

"I just had a talk with John Millinchamp and shared a bit of rum," Nate replied. "What are you up to?"

"Just checkin' on ya, Nate."

"You must be up to something! Look at that sunset, Henrietta. What a beautiful sight it tis. Ya don't see anythin' like that anywhere else in the world."

Laying down the basket of vegetables, Henrietta said, "Maria an' me taut you like ta have fresh beans, cabbage, an' sum fruit. We been givin' plenty food ta otha peopo, many peopo lose dea gardens from dem sons a beeches. Evr'body needs ta he'p."

Nathaniel's interest in Maria kept the villagers talking up a storm. This never happened before. No one had seen him so smitten. He paid no mind to the gossip, although Mama Henrietta kept him informed of all the talk.

"Mistah Nate, Mama know you long time, you no can fool Mama. I go now, but I be watchin' you. Pretty soon sumting gonna give, pretty soon."

"Now what's on yer mind? I know you too well, Henrietta, yer betta than a town crier, you know that?"

"Mistah Nate, dat's not nice. I on'y say wat is true, not pass bad talks. Oh. Okay, peopo keepa askin' me about you an' Maria. Wat's goin' on? dey asks me? So now, Mistah Nate, wat's goin' on?"

"Why, Henrietta, you do like to get right to the point, doncha? That's what I just love about you. What would we do without you? For yer information, not a thing! Now go, I have things to do."

Nathaniel watched as Henrietta walked toward her village. He thought, *these islanders, they have been after me to court Maria, they're manipulators. Well, they may be right, for she is quite smart, very pretty, and one of the toughest little gals I've ever seen anywhere. Henrietta is right, but I won't let her know. I have been taken with Maria since I first laid my eyes on 'er, but more than smitten, I cain't get over her spunk. By damn, that little thing gave Mazarro his comeuppance, she did. In spite of his cruelty, she had him by his jewels. Tough she is. I do respect the way she hunkered down. You had of thought she was a lot older than fifteen when she arrived here. Well, ole boy, looks like Mama knows betta than you about how you feel about someone! Hmmm! I wondah if Maria would want to return to Guam with the Millinchamps? Betta ask her meself. Didn't think about that when John was here. Hmmm!*

Love Revealed

N ATHANIEL visited Maria shortly after Henrietta questioned him about his intentions toward Maria and pondered, *Why does she want to know how I feel about Maria? What do I have in mind? Damn! I don't know. Ye will know in time, Henrietta…when I know.*

Now Nate felt the urgency to visit and talk to Maria. In all his conversations with her, they never spoke about Guam. So, he decided this was the time to broach the subject. He needed to know for himself and hoped she would not want to return, but her answer was very important to him and wondered where she stood. *I am curious. Had she heard that Joaquina and Millinchamp were returnin' to Guam on the* Portsmouth? *Would she want to return to Guam too?*

Maria had just put the children down for the afternoon and ran into Nathaniel as she headed to the garden. With a broad smile, she said, "What a nice surprise, Nathaniel. Out for your daily inspection?"

"Oh no, I came to see you, Maria. My day is not complete if I don't see you," he answered shyly.

"How nice to hear that, Nathaniel. I, too, feel my day moves very slowly when you don't come around."

Nathaniel smiled upon hearing Maria's response and said, "I assume that ye have heard that Joaquina and Millinchamp will be returnin' to Guam when the *Portsmouth* sails in a fortnight. I am wonderin' if ye might be wantin' to return to your home and parents as well."

"Why are you so concerned, Nathaniel?" Maria responded. "No, I cannot return to my home and parents with the Millinchamps, who tricked me into coming here. No one, not my father, not anyone looked for me. I don't believe anyone really cared. Bonin is my home now, the people care for me here, and I love them for that. This is where I have grown up, and I will die here. I need not say more. Thank you for asking, Nathaniel!" Shaking, she turned and entered her shanty.

Stunned at the sudden change in Maria, Nathaniel shouted, "Don't go, Maria. I am so happy to know ye want to remain here! I cannot tell you how you make me feel, Maria. Please come out so I can express my feelings for you." Thinking, *Sure got meself in a muddle of fish, now what do I do? She's one fiery lady, whew! What have I done? Now I know where she stands, and I know I love this woman. My god, Savory, you fool, you spoiled the best chance you will have with this wonderful girl.*

Maria, perplexed, thought, *what is he up to? He never talked to me about my relationship with Joaquina and Millinchamp, and now he's asking me if I want to return to Guam with them. No, no, no, never… especially after he expressed how his day isn't complete until he sees me. Is he trying to get rid of me? He can't be! Maybe I have to flirt with him more…be the siren that awakens him like nothing has before. Maybe that's what I have to do. When I hear his voice, my heart beats fast, and when I see him in the distance, every pore of my body reacts. I have never felt like this before. I look forward to hearing his voice, seeing him work with the islanders. He makes me feel whole, and yet…can't he see how I feel? For months, I have had strange dreams about him. Some of my dreams awaken me, they are so real. One of the dreams is the same as all of the dreams I have been having about Nathaniel and me. My dreams have not changed since I started having them. Nathaniel comes to me in the night when all are sleeping, he quietly crawls into bed with me and touches my body all over. Madre Mia! He drives me crazy. Just as suddenly as the dream appears, I awaken alone. What happened? I do not know what love is, but maybe what I feel is love. Now he is trying to get rid of me. No, Mr. Savory, it will not be easy, this girl is staying right here. I have made a life here for my children and me.*

The next few days, both Maria and Nathaniel tried to stay busy, but Nathaniel could not keep his mind on anything else but Maria and her reaction to his question about Guam. *What a fool I've been,* he kept saying to himself over and over. *I can't get any work done, and everyone is asking me for something. I hafta tell Maria how I feel. She has ta know and right away. I cannot let another day go by without explaining why I asked.*

Maria and Hanna had their hands full with the gardening and the children, along with the day-to-day happenings. Mama Henrietta needed their help with a villager who needed the dressing to his wounds changed, a fisherman who had a battle with a huge shark. Even though the shark lost the battle, the man nearly lost his arm. The shark, though, made a meal for many of the islanders.

Still Hanna kept asking if Nathaniel had been around. Maria's response was an emphatic no. Mama Henrietta had seen Nathaniel and noted that he, too, was short of temper. *Sumting preety fishy wid dese two. Betta nosey round an' find out. Right now, dis no good.*

Early one evening, after bathing the children and putting them to bed, Maria was startled by a knock on her door. There stood Nathaniel on the porch nervously turning his hat in a circle.

"Nathaniel! What?"

"Maria, please don't close the door. I came to tell ye something I should have told you a long time ago, but I wasn't sure you would hear me. Now I have to chance it.

"Maria, I am so happy that you want to stay here on Bonin. I realize now what I wanted you to hear from me, and what I wanted to hear from you. I love you more than I have ever thought I could love someone. You are someone I want to live with the rest of my life. You are a young woman, and I am many years older than you, but when I am around you, I feel young and happy. Do you understand what I mean, Maria?"

Surprised by Nathaniel's confession, Maria was happy to know the answer to her heart's question. She stepped onto the porch and said, "Oh, Nathaniel," and snuggled into his arms. He wasn't quite sure what to do, but she knew and quietly but firmly pulled his head down to her and kissed him with the deep feelings her dreams brought to her every night.

The two held on to each other for quite a long time.

About that time, Mama Henrietta and Hanna started around the corner of the shanty, but stopped suddenly. Mama slapped her hand over Hanna's mouth and vigorously shook her head no. They stood for a moment, stared, and slowly stepped away, leaving the two lovers to themselves.

Maria thought she heard Mama Henrietta's voice but paid no mind to it. Henrietta could not contain her joy and began laughing, talking, and singing all at once. Hanna thought Mama had simply gone crazy, but no, Mama was just beside herself with happiness for the two people she dearly loved.

"Dis berry good," she commented to no one in particular.

The Wedding Plans

NATHANIEL'S boisterous response to Maria's acceptance of his marriage proposal awakened Arita. She sat up rubbing her eyes, and then in awe watched her mother and Savory as they danced round and round. At the same time, Johnny Boy ran around in circles shouting, "Mama, mama!" Everyone danced, so Arita clapped her hands and wiggled her body in her own little dance too.

When the excitement died down, Nathaniel said, "Maria, my love, when do we marry? Right now, would be me choice."

Maria shook her head. "No, I want to marry in a real ceremony, with a priest or a man of God, Nathaniel, and our banns of marriage must be announced every Sunday for three weeks. How can we do these things?"

Nathaniel, surprised at her request, answered, "With no formal church on Bonin, it will be difficult to be married in a church, and we need a church to formally announce the banns of marriage, don't we?"

Maria replied with a shrug of her shoulders, "I don't know. If any man can, you can, Nathaniel. I know you can make this happen."

Rubbing his chin and thinking, Nathaniel said, "I will have an answer before tonight. Maria, we will have the wedding you desire. I will do everything I can to make this happen, you have made me a happy man, me love.

Nathaniel headed back to the teahouse deep in thought. *First, I have to see what to do about the banns, and then I have to find someone who can perform the marriage. There could be one on a whaler or a barge comin' back from the Alaskan waters. I best hurry back to me house, check the manifests to see who will be returning to Bonin for fresh supplies. The manifests will have an answer.* Nathaniel, still deep in thought almost ran Mama Henrietta down.

Henrietta held her hands up and shouted, "Hey, hey, Nate what wrong wid you? Sumting wrong you not see Mama?"

"No, no, Henrietta, I didn't see you, my friend, I was so deep in thought. I am so sorry, did I hurt you?"

"Sumting Mama he'p you with, Nate? Erthing awright? Maria and babies, dey fine? Whatcha got up yer sleeve?"

Nathaniel started to answer Henrietta. Then he thought, *Who is the one person I trust on this island? Henrietta, a course, I trust her with my life. She could hear my problem, and without a doubt, she will have a solution, at least one.*

"I do need your advice, Henrietta. You see, I just asked Maria to marry me"

"Wat you say, Nathaniel?" shaking her head in disbelief. "You say Maria be your wife? You ask her dat? My, my, Nathaniel, wat takes you so long? Wat Maria says?"

"Maria said yes! But she wants to have a real marriage by a man of God, a person like a priest, she wants to have our banns announced before the wedding."

"She not want jus' you take her to yer house to live like ever'body do?" Henrietta asked in confusion. "Mama berry happy to heah you finally do dis. Good ting I not hold me breath, Nathaniel. Wat dis bann ting anyway?"

"We don't have a minister on Bonin, and we don't have a priest, but I have the authority as magistrate to perform a wedding ceremony just like I perform funerals. I have to wait for a barge or a whaler to sail in and ask the cap'n to perform the marriage for Maria an' me. The banns are given to all the people that a marriage is takin' place, the banns are announced for three weeks before the weddin', and if anyone objects, then they must come forward before the weddin'. You understand, Henrietta?"

"Much easy to do Bonin way. But evr'body be berry happy fo' you and Maria, you good peopo."

"Henrietta, you have any idea how we can announce these banns without a church?"

"Sur do, we taka conch shell lika we do to celebrate tings dat are good, an' we blow conch shell to da north, den da south, den da east, and west gods askin' um for dey blessings: Den for t'ree week, ever' time we blow da conch, we tell ever'body 'bout yer weddin'. Dis will bring dos mans who tink dis weddin' no good to say so, an' if no mans come, dat berry good. Dat will hep yer gods too, you tink?" Henrietta answered.

"Bless you, Henrietta, I wouldn't have thought of a conch shell. I believe Maria will like the conch too. Now all I need is for a ship to sail into Port Lloyd. Thank you, my friend."

Henrietta, besides herself with happiness, couldn't wait to leave and announce the good news to Hanna and everybody. She couldn't get her feet to move as fast as her mind. *Hafta talk to Maria, tell her we be helpin' her wid da weddin' ting. She not say nothin' 'bout Nate, not nothin', why she not tell Mama? Ohh, maybe she not know, maybe she too shy to tell how she feel for Mistah Savory. Oh, dis is a happy day, Mama hafta tell all da villagers. Nooo, not Mama! Maria, she say, betta dat way."*

Maria's Wedding Request

Aꜰᴛᴇʀ Henrietta left, Nathaniel pulled the more recent ships' manifests from the shelf. These records were his lifeline to the world. Just as he did on his own ship, he kept a log of everything seen or accomplished daily. This too kept him in tune to the outside world. Nathaniel knew all these sailors intimately, and they knew and respected him for his trustworthiness.

He kept a separate journal for the monies many of the captains left in his care, along with copies of their last will and testament. He had an impeccable reputation among the seagoing men as well as the merchants from the various islands with whom he did business. A trustworthy man, the captains knew their cash would be safe in Nathaniel's hands. Even if their crews went crazy and mutinied, he had the authority to act as the captains' agent. He would take care of their property in a fair manner making sure the heirs would receive their due.

Having all the information in these manifests sure won't bring a ship in when I need it. Where are these ships when I need just one, just one? He carefully read each entry—nothing, not one ship scheduled to return for two to three months. *Damn! There could be one we didn't see before headin' to the whalin' fields, better not give up hope. I hafta tell Maria tonight, maybe things will change. I know Maria will insist on a legal marriage before she and the children move into my house, so 'tis up to me to find a ship or a minister…or both.*

Returning to Maria's that evening, Nathaniel thought about the banns and the other conditions Maria placed on the marriage. *This little girl means to make this marriage stick. Comin' from Guam under Spain's rule rubbed off on her people, what with the Catholic padres and such. I never thought she followed the church, but there is something there, wanting banns and all.*

If this is what Maria wants, this is what we do, and we wait for a ship to sail into port. Best we talk about this though. Maria went through a bad time with Mazarro. I think her prayers need answering, and her wanting a real wedding by a priest or pastor should happen. She must have prayed and prayed for mercy. God answered this little thing. He gave her the strength to stay alive to fight this crazy salt when he was beating on her and doing terrible things. She is someone very special, and my own Ma would approve of our marriage, she would.

The children were fed, bathed, and in bed before Nathaniel's arrival. Maria wanted this evening to be a quiet one as she and Nathaniel had things to discuss. Maria wondered, *Am I asking too much of Nathaniel? Would he try to talk me out of either the banns or even finding a minister? I am little concerned, but if we try and find out we can't, then maybe we can think of another way. We will see, but I won't give up too easily, and he knows that. If I were still on Guam, my father would see that I would have a wonderful wedding. Well, I am not on Guam. I will have a true marriage to the man I love, with or without my family. No, I will not live without a marriage to bless the children we will undoubtedly have and for Johnny Boy and Arita's sake.*

Maria had prepared a meal for Nate. She thought, *He might be hungry.* She had a small mackerel, about five pounds, which she laid on a large banana leaf. She sprinkled it with sea salt and chopped some fresh peppers and garlic onto it, laid onion rings over the fish and squeezed freshly picked limes and grated coconut over the entire dish, then wrapped it tightly in the banana leaf tied with strips of copra and then placed it on the fire to steam. She sliced and grilled a plantain, added fresh coconut milk and a little fresh mint over the plantain—ready to serve.

As Nathaniel entered her yard, he could smell the mackerel steaming in its juices, and it made his mouth water. *Delicious,* he thought. *What smells so good? How lucky can one man be?*

She looked beautiful, her hair sending off lights of its own as she stood near the open flames, dressed in a brightly colored long skirt and a white top embroidered with a delicate white lace pattern, her raven hair woven with fresh gardenias in a thick braid that hung down her back. She had the stature of a queen. Stunned by her beauty, he stood there for a short time and savored what he saw. *My Paw kept asking why I didn't marry. I just did not have an answer. Now I know why. I waited for Maria, she would be the only one. She stole my heart. What a lucky man I am.*

Maria looked up and smiled when she heard him enter. Nathaniel's heart danced, telling him, *Hang on, man, she's got you!*

Maria started toward him, still smiling, and once again his heart almost jumped out of his chest. *She is excruciatingly beautiful! And I have to wait for a ship to come in before she will be mine. Torture, that's what this is, torture.*

Nathaniel, flirting with Maria, smiled at her and said, "What smells so delicious, could that be you?"

Maria laughed. "It's your dinner, sir, that's what smells good. And oh, we made pretty good beer, Mama Henrietta, Hanna, and I did. We started it a month or so ago, and today we had a grand time tasting it. It made us a little drunk, so we stopped. You'll like it too, I hope."

Maria took the fish off the fire, laid it on a wooden platter in the middle of the table, served rice, then scooped the fish onto a plate. She had made fresh tortillas, sliced an avocado, squeezed lime juice over it, and served Nathaniel, who could hardly wait to taste this food. Savoring every morsel as Maria watched patiently, waiting for his approval, he said, "You've been keeping your cooking a secret, haven't you? This is so tasty! You are quite a cook."

Maria grinned and said, "Thank you, I've been cooking since I was a little girl."

Nathaniel paused and said, "I had a big conversation with Henrietta regarding the banns. I will go to any length to make you happy!"

As they talked, Maria decided that waiting would give them both time to work things out. She looked at Nate and said, "It's too bad we both have taken so long to discover each other, but we know why. Mazarro!

"You know, Nathaniel, many ships sail into Port Lloyd by accident, maybe one or two a month, and maybe there will be ships coming back from the fields that didn't stop here for supplies. Wouldn't you think that one could sail into port on the return for whatever reason, the whaling season is not over yet?"

"You're right, but let me tell you how we will have the banns announced."

Impatient with Nathaniel's evasive answer, Maria interrupted him and replied, "So what do you think of the possibility of a ship running off course and finding Port Lloyd? It is possible, isn't it? When you answer that, then let's talk about the banns."

"Yes, it is possible, but we can't set our hearts on it, can we?" he responded.

"You're right, but we can still hope. In the meantime, I will plan our wedding."

Nathaniel shook his head. *This woman has me all tied up in knots already, and we have not said our "I do's." Betta get on the ball and make sure I have not missed a ship on the manifests I have.*

Straightening up after the meal, Maria turned and looked into Nathaniel's face. Not even thinking, she bent down, cupped his face into her hands, and gently kissed him—first, on his forehead; then his eyes; then his cheeks.

Surprised at what Maria did, Nathaniel took her into his arms and kissed her with such passion, it touched her core. Running his hands up and down her body, he wanted to whisk her away and lay her on a bed. Besides himself with emotion, never in his life had he felt such a love for any woman. Oh, he had women, lots of them, but never did he kiss anyone like he kissed Maria, nor loved a woman like he loved this beautiful young woman. Nathaniel felt a deep contentment. He had never felt so loved.

Maria had never been kissed, not like this, and yet she knew this was how she wanted her first romantic kiss to feel like, thinking, *Are all kisses like this? Oh my goodness, my whole body is tingling all the way to my toes and wanting more. Maybe we won't wait for a ship to sail into port.*

Both of them were shaking with emotion, neither wanting to stop, but Nathaniel said, "If I don't leave now…" Then just like that, he gave her a gentle kiss and left her without a word.

The Wedding Banns

S ITTING on a bench outside in the darkness, Maria still feels Nathaniel's kisses, wondering if this was just another dream. *Did this really happen?* Her body answered her question. *I feel weak down to my toes. Does a dream do that? Does it?* She hugged herself. Warm with the memory of her first real kiss, she squirmed. *Oh, Nathaniel, your kisses send chills up my body. How did you learn to do that? Oh, my goodness. For the first time in my life, you awakened something in me. Something deep within I never knew existed. I am so simpatico! Once Joaquina tried to explain this feeling, this desire, and I thought she made it up. Now I understand, and I think I know what Joaquina tried to tell me. For the first time in my life, I feel a strong desire to push myself at you. Hmmm…girls don't do that. Do they? How can a kiss make me feel this way? Oh, Nathaniel, if we can't find a ship, it will be all right if we follow the Bonin way!*

For the first time since Mazarro's death, she felt a calmness envelop her. With Mazarro, she was always on pins and needles waiting for the next assault. Her time with him kept her on guard, not knowing what would set him off. Even though Maria stood her ground with him, she was ready to act or react.

She smiled. *Nathaniel makes me feel safe and loved. I will be forever grateful to him for that. Now no matter what, my family will be well cared for. He is a man of his word. I have to share my good news with Mama Henrietta and Hanna. They will be crazy with happiness, especially Mama. I think she must have used her magic potions on Nathaniel. Goodness, she did give him a hard time. Exasperating as Mama can be, Nathaniel loves and respects her, so he takes her harassment lightly…most of the time.*

No sooner did the thought escape her head that there they were, Mama and Hanna, huge smiles on their faces, bringing heavenly scented leis to put around Maria's neck and one to wear on her head as a crown.

Hanna said, "In Ponape, da island weah I be borned, da wimmin wear on dea heads da leis like crowns. Dis good custom I keep to make Hanna happy wen Hanna tink of weah we come from. Hanna nevah forget, no nevah."

The two women, Mama and Hanna, were crying and laughing at the same time for this special girl whom they protected and loved. The three of them, brought together by circumstances beyond their control, became a family of their own making.

Talking and crying all at once, Mama raised her hand, tearfully saying, "Ya know, Maria, I wait long, long time fo' Nathaniel ta ask you. Dis man's a berry good man…he no chase afta wimmin, he no beats no ones, he berry kind to ever'body, even though some mans dey jealous heem, dey make tings bad for heem sometimes, even make plan to keel heem, but we take care of dat. Nathaniel he take care and treat his odda girls berry good. He no want ta marry dem though, he no ready.

"Now dis time is different. He wanna marry, he see you, and right away Mama know, you da one he goin' ta marry. Mistah Savory no mo have girls from da village…Mama maka shua dat. Hanna and me so happy fo' you an' da babies…so happy."

Surprised at what she heard about Nathaniel and that Mama felt the need to give her the before-marriage pep talk about Nathaniel and his ways, Maria thanked her for the information, even though she felt it wasn't necessary. *Nathaniel would have told me all these things before they married. It doesn't matter to me what went on before I entered the picture.*

Hanna, between tears and laughter, looked at Maria and asked. "How Mistah Savory tells you, Maria? Did he maka beeg talk or you say, Maria, time to get marry?"

"No, Hanna, Nathaniel just brought fresh oranges up to give to us and to talk. Then he wanted to ask me a question, so I said I would try to answer. Then he asked me, 'Would you honor me by becoming my wife?'"

Hanna said, "Dat wat he do? He brings fruit? Funny man, maybe betta den say noting right? Wat you say, Maria?"

"Well, I said, 'You surprise me, Nathaniel, are you sure?' He said, 'Very sure.' And then I said, 'I would be very happy to be your wife if you would take Johnny and Arita too.' He said, 'He would be honored to take the children, too.' So, I answered, 'Yes, yes, yes!' It made us all happy, and we started to dance, even the children. After a while, I put the children to bed so we could talk."

"Wat happen den?" Hanna asked.

"You are too curious, Hanna. Anyway, I said, 'If it is all right with you, then I want to be married by a priest or a man of God, and I want our banns of marriage announced for three weeks before the wedding.' He was surprised at my request, then he was quiet for a little bit. Then he answered me by saying, 'I know we have no priest or a minister here, but if this is what you want, then I will do my best to find a minister or a priest. You will have to give me a while to get the answers, would that be all right, Maria?' And I said, 'I could wait.' Nathaniel left and returned to his home but came back a little later and told me he had spoken to Mama about the marriage and the banns.

"Hanna and Mama, we need your help to plan our wedding. You are my family, will you help?"

The two women were beside themselves. They hadn't taken part in a wedding of any kind before, but Mama, of course, had some ideas. First, she had to ask some serious questions.

"Dat is very good of you, Maria, we be honored. But tell us why you not just be like da Bonin peopo, no need worry 'bout man of God or da banns or wat eva. Dey jus move in togedda."

"I always thought I would be married in the Dulce Nombre da Maria Cathedral in Hagatna where my mother and father were married, where I was baptized. In Guam, it is customary for the family of the bride to announce the upcoming marriage every Sunday for three weeks before their wedding date. This is done to protect the bride and the groom from any unwanted suitors or bad debt or anything that might go against the marriage. After the third announcement, the wedding can be blessed. Getting married by a priest is important to me. After the wedding, the bride and groom with their attendants and their families parade from the cathedral down the main streets to the bride's home for the reception or fandango. This is the custom in Guam, I just want to be married by a man of God and for the banns to be announced, and then I'll feel that we did the right thing, and our marriage will be blessed. Do you understand, Mama?"

"Yes, now I unnerstan. How ta do dis fo' you an' Nathaniel? He lookin' fo' a ship. Maybe he finds someone on ship can marry you. Dat his job. Our job, we figger out da banns, we no have catedal, but we have sky, stars, ocean, flowers. God make all dat, an' all we need is find a man of God. Our catedal berry beeg, so we need ta tink 'bout da banns an' heah how

"In country wheah I come from, eva time a good ting happen, a man blow da conch shell. Da conch shell berry sacred, dis job is berry speshol. Only speshol mans can blow hard fo' da gods ta hear. Dey make shua all da gods know 'bout da good news an' sumtime da bad news, so da mans he blow da conch shell ta gods in da north, he turns ta da gods in da east, den ta da gods in da south den to da gods in da west tellin' ever'body da news. Dis is good fo' us heah in Bonin, cuz all da gods are heah, and dey hear da banns. Dey watch ova us. Wat you tink 'bout dat, Maria?"

"Well, Mama, you do understand! Let us toast to Nathaniel, to me, and our good fortune. Here we are, toasting with beer, freshly made by three smart women!"

Maria poured some beer into each of their glasses, and they toasted to a well-planned wedding. As they drank, they talked about the banns, the attendance of course, and wondering if anyone would speak up against the marriage, and they prayed for a ship to come into port with a man of God on it. No matter how long it took, these three ladies would be ready.

The Wedding Dress

MARIA and her friends took care of the two children, drank and toasted the bride to be, and planned the wedding, or so they thought. Soon Maria announced there was no more beer and she was going to lie down for a while. Hanna and Mama Henrietta stumbled back to their shanty, singing and laughing, Mama Henrietta holding on to Hanna so she would not fall.

Mama slurred, "No way we drink too much beer, no way. Whatcha put in it, Hanna?"

"Noting, Mama, noting. We celebrate too much, dat wat we do. So you drink mo' beer dan me an' Maria. You too happy, you say so many, many time."

"Okay, okay," Mama argued, "so wat we do now?"

"Sober up, so we can tink. We hafta taka sumting to help us. It too early in day fo' go to bed. You lie down on porch, I make sumting good fo' us, ta hep us get betta, so we can tink."

Hanna then prepared a concoction of fish soup base and eggs, adding some strong peppers and a little of the beer that started all this.

"Wear you learn ta do dis crazy-lookin' drink, Hanna?"

"I dun no…someplace. We hafta tink 'bout da weddin', Mama, we hafta help Maria, Mistah Nate, he have beeg job to find ship wid a padre or a captain dat kin say da vows ta marry. Maybe we get lucky an everting come togetter…dat berry good."

While the two were nursing their huge hangovers in their shanty by the beach, Maria, in her shanty had a moment while the children napped and wrote several ideas on a tablet. She wanted desperately to remember everything. The children slept longer today, a good omen giving her a few private minutes to contemplate the demands she made for the wedding.

She thought, *How selfish of me to demand a priest or a man of God and then requesting that we also announce the banns of marriages. I wonder what Nathaniel thought. Then there is Mama Henrietta and Hanna, they all must think I am crazy. So maybe I better try to explain myself to Nathaniel. I certainly can make changes, and I will for his sake.*

She could hear Johnny singing to his sister and smiled as he sang while Arita tried to sing along. *How sweet,* she thought. *The only good thing Mazarro left were these two precious gems.*

Henrietta, feeling better after a short sleep, sat up, stretched, and smiled as she thought about the wedding. *Ahh! Mama knows wat to do. I hide bootiful china cloth ta make sumting speshol. Now, wat I do wid it? Dis maka bootiful dress for Maria, so betta start look in war me hides it.* She searched for bolts of fabric she kept for special occasions and turned everything upside down looking for the right roll of cloth.

When Hanna returned from the village, Henrietta asked Hanna if she remembered where she stashed the material in the first place. With an affirmative nod, Hanna showed Henrietta where she had put the cloth. Henrietta had carefully wrapped the huge bolt in a wax type of paper that came from China then wrapped it again in a clean canvas cover from one of the ships. She had it stored in a tightly fitted tin can used to keep dry foods safe from spoiling and from bugs.

Henrietta, feeling anxious, gently unwrapped the canvas revealing a beautiful bolt of silk, something she had saved for a long time for a special occasion. She gingerly unrolled the material and sighed when she could still feel the texture of this stunning silk and smell the fragrances of the Orient permeating through the wrappings.

Ahh! Dis is good, berry good for Maria's wedding dress, not true white but almost. Maria, she like, Mama know. Besides, Maria, she no virgin no more, she haf babies. Dis good color for her.

Meanwhile, Maria, Johnny, and Arita walked to the washing stream to bathe. Johnny loved playing on the bank of the stream as Arita scurried around the sandy beach with rocks close by. Johnny kept moving closer and closer to the mouth of the creek that flowed into the ocean. Maria turned to see him about to step into the ocean as the waves touched the shore. She knew that the merging of the creek and the ocean was a dangerous area, as strong whirlpools came from these waters flowing together and could drag a grown man under without warning. And Johnny knew this was not a playing place, as his mother had told him so many times before. When she shouted, "Johnny!" and ran to retrieve him, the little boy ran away from her.

"Dis fun, Mama! Come get me," Johnny shouted as his mother came closer.

"Johnny, you stop! Now!"

He tried to stop but tripped and fell into the rushing water, dragging him under.

Maria screamed, "Johnny, no! No!" He was struggling in the surf, swallowing the salt water. Maria did all she could to reach him before he was washed out to sea. She was able to grab him by the arm and pull him to safety. Johnny Boy was coughing and spitting out seawater and sand, screaming at the same time. Maria, shaking from what happened, held him tight, tears rolling down both of their faces. Holding him close, she carried him under her right arm on her hip. They returned to the wash area. Arita clapped her hands at the scene thinking this was a game.

Maria sat Johnny down next to Arita and explained why she had warned them about going near the water. Still shaken by his near accident, Maria grabbed her two children and held them tightly, quietly thanking God for being there to help her.

"Johnny berry sorrow, Mama, Johnny not 'member. I be a good boy, okay Mommy?"

"Mommy would be very lonely and sad if something bad happens to you or Arita. Mommy is not mad at you, she was just frightened."

"Okay, Mommy, you not be frightened no more. Johnny Boy not do dis again."

"Johnny and you, too, Arita, when Mommy tells you not to go near the ocean, she tells you because the ocean is dangerous for little children. There are currents in the ocean that can pull you under very, very fast. It is important to listen when Mommy or Tia Hanna or Mama Henrietta tells you no."

Maria sat with the children a long while, cherishing them. Then she said, "Mr. Savory and Mommy are going to get married. He wants to be your father. What do you think of that?"

Johnny clapped his hands and began to dance around his mother, shouting, "Yeah, Arita, we gonna be marry to Mistah Savory! Wat you tink?"

Arita, not understanding the meaning of all this excitement, joined in the celebration. Clapping her hands like her brother, she too danced around, smiling from ear to ear.

Maria was pleased with their happy responses, even though they were young and did not understand the full impact of the wedding announcement.

The little family returned to their home and, after getting some of their chores done, returned to the creek later to gather the dry clothes. The children ran ahead and bumped into Nathaniel. They hugged his legs, and Johnny Boy shouted happily, "We gonna marry you, Mistah Savory, dat is berry good, don' you tink?"

Nate, laughing at the announcement from Johnny, answered, "You betcha, it's a good thing. Now let's have a hug to seal this."

Announcing and Waiting

NATHANIEL was happier than he had ever been. He was certain of it, thinking, *my marriage to Maria will also bring two sweet little children into my life. It's more than I ever prayed for. I am a lucky man.*

As he walked back to his teahouse, he wondered why Maria thought the Bonin way would be better than waiting for a ship to sail into Port Lloyd. *Might be she doesn't think the ship will come. Worry ain't gonna bring one in, we'll see one before long. Well, I am glad she changed her mind. She'll be happy she did too. Now how do we accomplish the request for the banns when we have no wedding date?* he pondered. *We could announce the marriage, it will take three weeks. No surprise to me if a ship sails into our harbor within a fortnight. Therefore, we best start announcing the banns on Sunday next. Betta go back to Maria so we can choose our wedding day.*

Mama Henrietta and Hanna brought the bolt of fabric up to show Maria and talk about the dress they were going to design her wedding day. Maria, overcome with love for these two women who saved her life just two short years before, was thrilled that they came to her rescue once more with such beautiful fabric, a loving and generous gift, for her wedding dress. Overwhelmed by their love, Maria hugged them both and began to cry, "Oh, Mama, Hanna, thank you, thank you. This is so beautiful."

The three women discussed the design and how beautiful the color suited Maria's brown skin. She began to believe that the wedding would happen soon.

Now a young woman of seventeen years, the mother of two children born out of violence, she was ecstatic over finally finding love and looked forward to a marriage with a kind and respected man. In addition, she was talking to the dearest people in her present life, discussing her wedding dress. How happy she felt, finally free from all the abuse she experienced the past two years.

Shortly after the women left, Maria went to check on the little ones. Returning to the porch, there stood Nathaniel. Surprised, Maria smiled. "Nathaniel, I thought you were gone for the night."

"Maria, I have been thinking about the banns of marriage, and I didn't want to wait until morning to share my thoughts with you."

Maria couldn't wait to hear what he had to say, thoughts soaring in her mind, *My, this has been a full-of-surprises day and now more good news! First, Henrietta's gift, and now Nate has something important regarding our marriage.*

"Nate, what about the banns? Are we going to have them announced?"

Nathaniel answered with a huge smile on his face. "Of course, we will still announce our intent to marry. I was thinking that a ship might sail in before we announced our intent, and the ship might not be able to stay the three weeks it will take to complete the announcements. So, I think we should announce our intent right away, starting this coming Sunday."

"But, but, but," Maria blurted, "what if a ship doesn't come in, then what?"

Nathaniel put his hands on Maria's shoulders and, looking down at her sparkling brown eyes, said, "There are many vessels on the water, my love. Many are heading for the whaling fields. Many stop here at Port Lloyd for freshwater or fill their holds with fresh fruits and vegetables. We're bound to see a ship soon…within a fortnight, I would say."

She asked hesitantly, "Can we announce the banns and not marry right away?"

"I think so, but listen, I believe we'll see a vessel sail into Port Lloyd very soon, and I want to make sure the banns have been posted.

Then we will be ready when a ship comes to Bonin, be it whaler, merchant, or anything else. What do you think? Should we set our wedding date now, or should we just announce our intentions?"

Maria was overwhelmed with how quickly things had escalated, and she excitedly responded, "Can't we set a date then still announce the banns just in case a ship comes to port soon and change the date if we have to wait?"

"I believe we can. So, do you think we can announce our intents beginning on Sunday?"

"Is this the first week of the eleventh month of the year, Nathaniel?"

"Aye, aye, why do you ask?"

"If this is the first week, then let us plan on marrying on the fourth week, maybe the last day?"

"Aye, you are right, November 30, 1850, sounds good to me. You sure this is what you really want, Maria?"

"Oh, yes, yes! Thank you, Nathaniel, thank you." Running into his arms, she kissed him so passionately, he almost decided not to wait.

The Bonin way has its merits, he thought.

Things were beginning to get beyond his control. Feeling weak and vulnerable, he wondered, *What is going on? Why am I being so complacent? As a man and the magistrate of the island, I am letting a very appealing, sensual little girl worry over things like ships arriving and making sure we have three weeks to post the banns of marriage. I am not myself, and it gets in the way of running the island. She handles me like clay, molding me this way and that. I love it and do not care who knows. What has happened to Mistah Savory? Everyone is saying. And I will shout, Mistah Savory is in love! Oh, yes! I am in love!*

He kissed Maria good night, saying, "If I don't leave now, things may change. Let me go, my love, let me leave you now, please." Once again, he turned away. Maria knew what almost happened and watched as he left.

She, too felt as Nate did, softly saying, "Oh, God, please bring us a ship soon with a captain who can marry us."

Nathaniel decided to at least check on things, not wanting to return to the teahouse right away. He had much to think about. As he turned to go up toward the teahouse, Henrietta was checking things out herself. This helped her to sleep when she had things to work out in her mind. They saw each other and waved; then Henrietta yelled, "Nathaniel, wait!"

He stopped and waited for Henrietta to catch up to him. Breathing hard from her run toward this man that everyone looked up to, she blurted, "Aw right now! What go on wid you? There still no sheep. What go on? You nevah goin' marry Maria. Right? She da right one fo' you an' you know it, too. Why you wait an' wait?"

"Well, let me be the first to announce that Maria and I have decided to get married in November the last day. By that time, a ship will have come into port." Laughing, he added, "Are you satisfied now, Ms. Nosey? Oh, and do you have someone who knows how to blow the conch? We want to have our banns announced beginning this Sunday, for three Sundays."

Henrietta folded her hands and looking skyward prayed, "Ahieee, bless you, God, tank you, tank you. Yes, yes, yes! Now Mama betta get da dress started, an' tells da conch shell mans to be ready ta blow loud an' clear dis Sunday. Oh! Oh! Mama so happy fo' you an' so happy fo' Maria. Berry good job, Nathaniel."

Nate smiled broadly as he watched Mama run back to her village to excitedly announce the good news. Everyone in the village, even some of the old sailors who lived among the natives, came out to hear what Mama had to announce.

Hanna ran after Mama, yelling, "Mama, Mama, wat happening?"

"You not know dat Maria haf a wedding day. We hafta sew dah dress pritty fast. Need to get conch blower to blow for dah banns."

Henrietta was beside herself with a joy she had not felt in years and years.

On this island of Bonin in the year 1850, all the inhabitants were excited about this special celebration. That first Sunday, Nathaniel, Maria, and the two children, dressed in their finest, paraded down to the harbor. There, one of the Hawaiian men stood on the highest point of the beach. He put the conch to his mouth, turned and faced the north, and blew to the gods of the north, then turned to the south and blew to the gods of the south, turned slowly toward the east and blew the conch to the gods of the east, then toward the west, assured that the gods were happy. He turned and walked slowly away.

Henrietta moved toward the center of the beach, turned to the villagers, and announced in her best voice, "Senores y Senoras, dis is da numbah one of tree announces fo' dah marriage of Nathaniel Savory ta Maria da los Santos y Castro. Anybody no like dis marriage den you haf two more Sunday to say so, an' Mama say nobody betta say nuttin."

Nathaniel looked down and winked at Maria when he heard Mama's threat. Maria looked at Nathaniel and smiled thinking, *No one has ever winked at me. I wonder what it means.*

Nearly everyone on the island was present for the announcement, the first of its kind to his or her knowledge. When Henrietta finished this first special announcement, they all clapped and hooted their approval. Hanna seemed to be the loudest.

Henrietta turned and looked at the little family she loved so much. Nathaniel shook hands with all the men, and Maria had an ear-to-ear smile on her face. Johnny and Arita hung on to Maria and Hanna, happy too at all the excitement.

The next Sunday, everyone gathered once more at the harbor, witnessed the ritual of the conch shell, and heard Henrietta make the formal announcement and threat…only this time her threat ended with "Mama, she see ever'body, if ya knows wat good fo' you."

Nathaniel thanked Mama for her announcement but suggested that she should not threaten anyone adding, "Maria and me, we want our marriage to go well. So promise not to threaten anyone, please."

Henrietta thought she was doing the right thing, but she understood, thinking, *well no one showed up, so dat is good.* "Awright, Mama promise."

Hanna, Henrietta, and Maria worked daily on the dress, and by the last Sunday, it was finished. Excitement permeated the two shanties. Every stitch on the wedding dress was hand sewn by one or the other women. The women of the beach were busy weaving baskets and other gifts they were going to give to the couple.

The men of the island watched the sea for any sign of a ship. Every day that they fished out in the ocean, they watched for signs of sails heading toward Bonin. The weather was changing. It would not be long before someone spotted a sail. One of the whalers would be returning soon filled to the brim with whale oil, bones, and other things…and, hopefully, announcing a sign of sails on the horizon.

Will a stray ship sail by? Everyone watched the sea for a sign. There seemed to be varied opinions as to why no ship came near or how many times someone shouted "Sail Ahoy" to be an illusion. Nathaniel remained optimistic that one would arrive.

The Fiesta for the Banns

THE third week of the banns was slowly creeping up and still no ship in sight. Maria did not worry; she had the feeling that before the third Sunday, a sail would be spotted. However, Nathaniel began to wonder if he had miscalculated.

In the meantime, everyone kept busy, many working to make this event memorable for all. This was in fact the biggest and most positive event since anyone could remember. A few years earlier, this island experienced the largest typhoon in many years and an earthquake that would always remind the Boninites how fragile their world was and how they survived it. Then the most recent destruction reaped on them by pirates, so much loss and for no reason except too much drink and meanness on the part of those desperadoes. What havoc they wrought! Therefore, by rights the Bonin people believed they truly deserved to celebrate what was good in their lives.

On Saturday, the weather was changing. Nate thought, *With these gusty winds, a storm might be brewing. We work around it if we have to. Maria won't mind, I know.*

Therefore, plans for the celebration continued. Hanna and Maria watched over the activity and jumped whenever needed. Arita and Johnny played nearby, watching the adults running here and there, singing, laughing, and making suggestive jokes about the coming marriage. They noticed how embarrassed their mother acted, but she, too, joined in the fun, so the two little ones adjusted to this unusual display.

Out of the corner of her eye, Maria kept watch over her well-behaved children. She saw that the other children were playing quietly as well, so she was happy. In a short time, she would be married to a good and honorable man, and she vowed to make Nathaniel happy he married her. She closed her eyes for a moment and silently said a prayer of thanksgiving, *God, you placed huge obstacles in my path to strengthen me, and now I know you prepared me for my life, my life here on Bonin. I thank you, Father in heaven.*

Henrietta and some of the beach village women planned a fiesta for the third announcement of the banns. Some men of the village brought in wahoo, a tropical fish of the mackerel family. Others killed a two-hundred-pound green turtle. Still others killed and prepared a kid goat for grilling the next day, a large wild pig killed three days before now baking in the ground. The women prepared fruits, vegetables, and other foods, everyone busy with one task or another.

Excitement filled the air…talking, singing, and telling of risqué jokes about men and women, so no one seemed to pay attention to the winds whipping up on the sea. No one, except, of course, Nate Savory who was concerned about this unexpected storm. *Maybe it will go away. I cannot do anything about it, can I?*

Sunday, everyone awoke to sunshine, even Nathaniel. He was much relieved that the storm passed them by. He was looking forward to standing next to Maria and the children while Henrietta announced the banns for the third and final time. With this announcement, he knew that he and Maria would marry, or at least be free to marry when a vessel came into port.

By 1100 hours, the villagers had gathered once again to witness the blowing of the conch, to hear the announcement, and especially to see if anyone would step forward to voice their objection. No one did, and Henrietta thought it was because of the warning she gave: "Nobody betta say notin'."

Maria thought, *Henrietta and her warning will become a joke between Nathaniel and me for many years to come!*

After the announcement, Henrietta invited everyone to the village for a special feast. Nathaniel and Maria, along with the children, draped in flowers, paraded to the fiesta.

What a wonderful day this turned out to be, especially since the storm that worried me never materialized, Nathaniel thought. *The unpredictable weather conditions we have here in the North Pacific should not be a surprise. Only a fool takes the sea for granted.*

The women of the village loved to party. No matter what the occasion, any excuse to celebrate. This celebration meant that the one man they all looked up to with respect and love was taking himself a wife whom they loved and cared for as well. The villagers knew the gods of the universe had blessed them more than ever with their honoring of this couple. All of the villagers, the men and women, even the cast-off sailors from different ships who now lived in the village, celebrated this day.

Maria and Nathaniel were happy even though they had to wait for a ship captain, a minister whom they did not know, to arrive and perform their ceremony. Everyone hoped that a ship would arrive in the next few weeks. Maria and Nathaniel had taken a vow of celibacy until their wedding night, so both of them were anxious for the wait to end. Everyone was anxious, all the villagers wondering what the two lovers were waiting for and not understanding why they did not live together like everyone else did, as no one had to tell them it was okay. The natives were definitely puzzled with this custom.

Maria could not come close to Nathaniel without a desire to make mad passionate love with him. Nathaniel wanted her so much he had to leave her presence after her desirable kisses left him weak and vulnerable. She, reconsidering her request for a real marriage, almost capitulated several times. Mama Henrietta thought this craziness should stop and get on with the mating game like any sane man and woman would do, but no, *Wat wrong wid dese two, dey maybe like ta suffa? Dea betta be a schooner or sumting come in soon!*

At Long Last, a Ship

AFTER celebrating the final announcement of marriage between Nathaniel and Maria, all the villagers kept their eyes peeled for signs of sails heading their way. Nathaniel had spotters in strategic places, and the fishermen, on their daily sail for halibut and other fish, watched for any sign.

Finally, almost ten days after the banns were announced, a ship was spotted from a mountaintop lookout, and word by a spotter was excitedly transmitted by shouts of joy; "Me sees a sail, comin' dis way, maybe dis is da one we wait for!"

Nathaniel sighed, *Finally…this wait has been a hard one for sure.* He peered through his spyglass to verify what country's flag the ship sailed under. *Aye, this is perfect, an American whaler. Now this is almost worth the wait. I must go to Maria to give her the good news.*

Looking through his spyglass as the canoes guided the ship into the harbor, Nathaniel focused on the whaler. The name stood out. "*No Duty on Tea*, hmmm…must be a story here," he uttered. *Well, no matter,* No Duty on Tea, *you have a wedding to perform on your deck. This is a happy day!*

Hearing the news, Hanna was beside herself with excitement and ran to tell Mama Henrietta. "Mama, Mama, a ship she comes, has American flag, dis is good. Is good we finish Maria's dress in plenny time…is berry good."

Nathaniel reached Maria's shanty just as she and the children were returning from the bathing place. Nathaniel ran up to Maria, grabbed her around the waist, and danced in a circle, Maria laughing at what he was doing, so unlike him to be so spontaneous. The children danced around their mother, as they often did with Nathaniel present.

"Maria, a ship has arrived, it is an American whaler, and her name is *No Duty for Tea.* Don't know who the captain is, but no matter. What do you think, Maria, are yah ready to be me bride?"

"Nate, we've waited so long, I don't want to wait another minute."

"That's my girl." Nathaniel laughed. "We need to speak with the captain as soon as he comes to shore. In the meantime, better talk to Henrietta, let her know not to go crazy. I am on my way to greet the sailor sent from the ship to request permission to debark here. You want to join me?"

"No, Nathaniel, you take care of the arrivals, and I will take care of the children. They will need a nap. There is much to do if this ship is where we are to be wed, but I cannot wait to hear the news and the plans you have made with the captain!"

As Nathaniel walked down to the shoreline, some of the men of the village joined him. They were always available when a ship sailed into Port Lloyd. As the group approached the dingy, Nathaniel shouted a hearty "Welcome to Port Lloyd!"

The young sailor stood at attention on the dingy and shouted, "Thank you, sir, I have been sent by our cap'n, Master Daniel McAdams, to request permission to anchor here at your port and permission to come ashore."

"What is the purpose of your request, sir?" Nathaniel asked.

"We've been at sea for three months and ten days, sir. We have two crew members in sickbay, they need more than we have for them, and our doc seems ta think they need dry land for a while. Cap'n McAdams wants to stay in port for a couple days so as we can get our whaler ready for the cold weather. Would this be an inconvenience for you and your people, sir? Also, sir, might ye be Nathaniel Savory, sir, or if not, are ye familiar with the person, sir?"

"I am Nathaniel Savory. What business would this vessel be haven' with me?"

"It's a pleasure, sir. Well sir, the cap'n has a packet of letters for ye. Wherever we stopped for freshwater and rest from the sea, it was pure seaman knowledge where our whaler was headed, and we would have to harbor here in Bonin before heading to the fields. So, with that, they asked our cap'n to carry letters and such to you. We have quite a lot of reading for ye, sir."

"Welcome to Bonin, and it will not be an inconvenience, we will gladly fix you up, as you still have a long journey ahead of you. Your cap'n McAdams is an American? What port do ye sail from?"

"We sail out of New Bedford, Massachusetts, sir. Our cap'n is from Maine, sir. Most of the crew comes from New England, some from Europe, some from the Sandwich Islands. We picked up the European sailors in 'Frisco, some place that Frisco!"

"Ah, New Bedford! Son, please extend my welcome to your captain, inform him that he and his crew are welcomed here. I too am from New Bedford, and it is a pleasure to welcome one of my countrymen."

"Yes sir! Captain McAdams will be glad to receive your invitation. Where can he find you, sir?"

"Just tell the captain to come to the teahouse, that's where I'll be."

The young sailor saluted Nathaniel. "Aye, sir!"

Nathaniel stood there for a while watching the dingy as it headed for its ship then turned and headed for his teahouse to prepare for Captain McAdams's arrival.

Captain Daniel McAdams

NATHANIEL prepared himself for Captain McAdams's visit and the captain's answer about the marriage that could take place aboard his ship. Since he was not acquainted with the captain, asking him to perform a marriage aboard his ship would be presumptuous. He was curious about the captain as surely as the captain was about him. Where did he sail out of, what harbor? In spite of his curiosity, Nathaniel was happy to know that McAdams was an American, sailing on an American vessel.

The teahouse was the meeting place for all the visiting ships captains and for the Boninites as well. It was the official government house as this was where the magistrate resided.

A short time later Nathaniel warmly greeted Captain McAdams as he came ashore. The two men found that New Bedford was their common ground. Once established, they talked about the happenings in the New Bedford and the Providence area while they shared homemade rum on Nate's back porch. This sailor was no greenhorn. He had been sailing a long time, had a lot of sea experience, and Captain McAdams commanded a great deal of respect from his crew.

After the small talk, Nathaniel felt comfortable with McAdams and said, "Cap'n, ye sailed into our harbor at a very auspicious time. The people here would say that the gods of the sea and the wind brought you here to us at this particular time."

"What do you mean by that, Mr. Savory?"

"First, please call me Nate or Nathaniel. Secondly, I have proposed to a beautiful lady from the island of Guam, a widow with two young children, and she has accepted my proposal of marriage but with some conditions…one being that the marriage must be performed by either a man of the cloth, of whom we have none, or a ship captain who can perform marriages. We have waited for a ship to sail into Port Lloyd for nearly a month and not a sign. During this month, the villagers have been working towards a wedding fiesta and have never let up on their prayers to their gods. The first shout of a sail in sight sent them into joyous frenzy. Believers and unbelievers alike knew that their prayers were answered, and to make it even more believable your ship flew the Stars and Stripes. What an omen!"

"The second condition of her acceptance to my marriage proposal is that my love and I would remain celibate until our weddin' night, so you see where I'm heading, Cap'n?"

"Definitely Nate, I certainly do!"

"Cap'n McAdams, do you have the authority to marry me an' me bride aboard your whaler *No Duty on Tea* today?"

"Well, sir, I do have full authority to marry couples on board. Saying that, I have something to discuss with you that's of great importance to our crew. We have two very sick crew members on deck that definitely need medical help. From what I understand, there are no doctors here, but do you have someone who acts as a medicine man? Taking care of my two men is a priority at the moment. Then we do a bit of house cleaning and after that I'd be honored to marry you and your bride. Ye do know we will need to sail three miles out to sea, don't you? I'd say we push for day after tomorrow. What do you think, Nate?"

"We would have liked the weddin' to be today, but what's waiting one more day. I think we can handle it. Maybe the others will not like it, but we will see. Of course you and the crew are invited to the festivities after the wedding and we return to shore. You can start moving those sick sailors off the ship. In the meantime, I will talk to Henrietta about their care. Then I will tell Maria we have about a day or so before we can marry. I am sure she will not mind. Captain

McAdams, it is a pleasure, sir, to make your acquaintance, and I am deeply grateful that you can and will perform the wedding ceremony."

Captain McAdams asked, "How long have ye been on this island, Nathaniel?"

"About twenty years, and I'm one of the five original settlers."

"Are you the only one who stayed?" the captain asked. "Where are the others now?"

"Let me see. There was John Millinchamp, Matteo Mazarro, Alden Chapin, Charles Johnson, and me. Millinchamp and Mazarro are British, even though Mazarro is from Genoa originally. Johnson came from Denmark, Chapin and me are from Salem and New Bedford, Mass. We also brought with us about twenty-five Kanakas. Out of that group were five women, we needed them for pleasure and to work for us. They kept us a little sane, if you know what I mean. To answer your question about their whereabouts, well, Charley Johnson, he left first, and then I heard he got himself murdered. Then Chappy, he got sick and died, he is buried right here on the island. Both he and Charley were good men. Mazarro was an evil person, of very mean character…bad in and out. Millinchamp and Mazarro traveled back and forth to Guam and other islands for trade and to bring needed supplies…flour, corn, rice, seeds, fruit, and such for our survival. They did all the sailing and the trading. I remained here to watch over the fort, so to speak."

McAdams eyes lit up. "Say, on my trip here, I heard in 'Frisco about this Mazarro person. Nothing good said about that man. All kinds of tales of stolen goods and captured women he would sell into Chinese brothels. His cruelty preceded him it seems. How did you make his acquaintance?"

"We all met in the Sandwich Islands, all of us there for various reasons. I was recuperating from an accident aboard my last ship and was hearing stories about uninhabited islands to explore and settlements we could start. Mazarro and Millinchamp were able to procure a British-owned ship we could use, especially for exploration and settling under the British flag. So the five of us pooled what cash we had and began our adventure."

The captain asked, "The young woman you are marrying, is she one of the original Kanakas who came with your party?"

"Oh! Not this little girl. Mazarro kidnapped her under false pretenses from the island of Guam. Her aunt Joaquina, who married Millinchamp, had a hand in it. When Maria found out, she never spoke to her aunt or Millinchamp again. After arriving here on Bonin, Mazarro forced her to live with him and eventually caused the birth of two children. Maria lived under his authority until he died a year ago. Her name is Maria da los Santos y Castro from Hagatna, Guam. Just fifteen years old when Mazarro took her and brought her here to Bonin. Maria is a tough little jewel. She fought him for her life and finally broke him down. He was not an easy man to have around and never had one true friend. I knew he was a sick man but no idea he suffered from syphilis, and it finally took him. Sometimes God blesses us."

"That's quite a story, Nate. You are a legend to every man I have encountered along this journey to the fields, even some of my own crew know about you. I've been told you are one honest man to do business with, so, it's a pleasure, sir, to meet you. Best I leave now to prepare for my first weddin' aboard my ship, could be a good omen for the *No Duty on Tea*."

The two men shook hands and arranged to meet in the next day for the long-awaited wedding of Nathaniel and Maria.

Let me see, it is 1000 hours according to my watch, Nathaniel pondered. *Maria and I have a few hours to prepare. Better see Henrietta, tell her what is going on regarding the sick sailors and the wedding. Have to give Maria time to dress and get the children prepared for the event. Better hurry, don't have much time. Hmmm, maybe Maria has most of this already figured out knowing how organized she is. I am a lucky man to have her in my life. Maybe I had better give her the lead when it comes to things of which I have no understanding.*

While Nathaniel was meeting with McAdams, Maria was taking care of the logistics of the family. She and Hanna had worked out a plan regarding the wedding on board the Yankee whaler.

Maria wanted Hanna and Mama Henrietta to be present on board the ship as witnesses for their wedding and knew she needed to tell Nathaniel of her decision. Feeling confident that he would go along with the plan, she went about preparing for her wedding. Johnny Boy and Arita would also be present. She would then have what she considered her family as witnesses. Nathaniel arrived at Maria's home as she was putting the final touches on the lei she would present to him.

"Nathaniel, what are you doing here? I thought you were with Captain McAdams?"

"I just left him, my love. He had some things to do on his whaler before he can marry us. He needs to take care of two sick sailors, get them off the ship for medical aid. He asked if we could put off our marriage until tomorrow. I said one more day would make no difference so long as we can marry. I hoped you would understand. You do, don't you?"

"You are right, Nathaniel, one more day won't make a difference, and we have a lifetime ahead of us. I must tell Mama Henrietta and Hanna though. Oh! I asked them if they would stand up for us as witnesses to our marriage. I hope you won't mind. They have been my family for the years I have been here…my only family."

"No, my love, I don't mind. It is a good idea to have them witness for us.

The Wedding

THE next morning, everyone in the village prepared for the wedding reception. Long tables, sitting about twelve inches off the ground, were set up for the guests to eat from. Mats were placed around all the tables for guests to sit at while eating, talking, and singing.

Huge fronds of the coconut tree were placed on the tables; then sweet-smelling flowers of all kinds were scattered over the fronds. The women were happy with their work; all of them had something to say through song about the couple's first night. Someone would start the song, and then another would add her vision of the first wedding night. After each verse, the women would laugh in a naughty way, especially as the verses became very descriptive.

The next morning, as 1000 hours approached, Nathaniel boarded the ship ahead of his bride and her Bonin family. He would meet his Maria on board the whaler. He wanted to watch as she sailed toward the ship. *This will be as perfect as if she walked down the aisle of a church,* he thought.

Watching the skiff carrying his bride, his soon-to-be adopted children, John and Arita, accompanied by Hanna and Mama Henrietta, Nathaniel's heart filled with emotion, something he hadn't felt all of his life.

Captain McAdams stood silently next to Nathaniel waiting for him to speak first.

Nathaniel turned and said, "I've never felt like this before, this feeling of joy that washes over my body. Watching her sailing toward us, her veil blowing about her beautiful face, just makes me quiver with emotion. What a lucky man I am."

"Aye, Nathaniel, 'tis a beautiful and moving picture for me as well."

Maria, fighting the veil and staring ahead at the whaler, had tears in her eyes as she thought about the true love she had for this gentleman she was about to marry. Mama Henrietta tried to be cheerful, but she too felt the emotion over the happiness she knew would come with the marriage of this very special couple, and she shouted into the breeze, "Dis day a berry good day fo' all us Bonin peopo. A berry good day!"

Once they were piped on board, Nate introduced Captain McAdams to Maria and the rest of the party. Cap'n McAdams escorted the bridal party to his cabin, as they set sail for the open sea and said, "Once the ship reaches the three-mile mark, the wedding party will proceed to the deck for the ceremony."

Although this ship was larger than the *Portsmouth*, Maria had not been on board a ship since her kidnapping. She felt uneasy until Nathaniel walked into the captain's quarters. He had a feeling she needed comforting.

A short time later, the captain called for the couple and the small family on deck. The crew had prepared a tarp cover to protect the bridal party from the breeze and spray. Captain McAdams stood in the center as one of the sailors played the bridal march on his harmonica and another accompanied him on a hand accordion. Mama Henrietta, Hanna, and the children stood in a half circle as the bride and groom walked the short distance to stand before the captain to take their vows of marriage.

Hanna and the children were excited. Once the captain pronounced the couple man and wife, Johnny and Arita shouted, "Yeah! Mistah Savory finally marry us…yeah!"

Maria took the lei she had created, put it over Nate's head, and kissed him. Not to be outdone, Nathaniel, after he slipped a gold wedding ring on her finger, placed a lei around Maria's neck and gave her a most passionate and loving kiss, whispering, "Now we are truly one, my love, you honor me by becoming me wife."

Back on shore, the natives were getting restless but remained polite. The women would not let the men drink, but they, too, needed the party. Everyone wanted to celebrate this marriage. The skiff returned with the newlyweds, and once their feet touched the shore, the festivities began.

The bride and groom had arrived. And with their arrival, an exciting parade, drums began beating, as the harmonica and hand accordion players led the bride and groom from the dock to the reception. The guests shouted their congratulations to the newlyweds as they entered. This party would go on all night. Henrietta started the night off with a toast to the couple; it was long as Henrietta's toasts always were. Finally, Nathaniel stood and thanked everyone who helped, especially Henrietta, Hanna, and the *No Duty on Tea* for sailing into port and bringing Cap'n McAdams with them.

He exclaimed, "A fine day this is for the Savory clan. I am the happiest man. Why? Because this most beautiful and wonderful woman has become me wife. Carry on, me friends, we are beholden to all of ye for yer friendships an' yer loyalty. Maria and me thank you from our hearts…thank you!"

The festivities went on and on through the night—lots of eating, lots of drinking, lots of laughter, lots of dancing and singing. Everyone suffered through the wait with this couple even if it seemed strange; they put so many restrictions on themselves. These two beloved people were special, and in the Bonin way, maybe dis way moh betta.

Nathaniel had a surprise for Maria. When they found the time to leave the party without being missed, he took her to their special place where he built a romantic lean-to covered in sweet-smelling flowers, candles, and a soft bed made up of many animal skins and the soft down of the wild goats.

Stunned by all the planning he went through and the love he wove into this lovely setting, she said softly, "Nathaniel, did you do this alone? Where did you find the time? I love it!"

"Yep, every day I would bring something up here, work with it, and imagine how you would feel about it. I want to give you something wonderful you will always remember about our Bonin. Starting here seems like a good beginning, don't you think?"

"How clever you are, my sweetheart. With you, Nathaniel, I have finally found the love I haven't felt in a very long time. I feel secure and cared for through your love. I will love Bonin so much more now that you are in my life. This is so romantic, Nathaniel! Thank you."

"I thought we needed to have time alone, especially tonight. If we stayed at the teahouse, someone would come. If we stayed at your shanty, we would have everyone, drunk or sober, show up. Here, this is ours, we can be ourselves, alone for one time."

That night they made love repeatedly with more passion each time. Nathaniel thanked Maria for becoming his wife, and she in return thanked him with more love than he ever felt in his lifetime. She knew how to please him and pledged to do so forever.

A Growing Family

A FTER their wedding night, Nathaniel suggested that they begin their married life at Maria's shanty. Maria said, "No, your business and your life is at the teahouse, we will use the shanty as a place to relax." So, Maria and the children moved into the teahouse.

A few weeks after the wedding and after settling into the teahouse, Maria announced to Nathaniel that she was with child. Nathaniel was beside himself with joy, anxiety, fear, and wonder all at once. She explained that she would be fine. He shouldn't worry. After all, she already gave birth to Johnny and Arita. Here was Nathaniel's seventeen-year-old wife consoling him, a forty-seven-year-old man. He mused, *My first child, and my lovely wife is telling me not to be concerned! I must get used to this fact. How my life has changed since Maria entered my heart.*

"Aren't you happy, Nathaniel?"

"I am very happy…just a little anxious I guess. I have never had a child before, and I am an old man. Am I too old to be a father?"

"Too old! Oh, Nathaniel, you are not too old. You'll be a good papa to our own. See how well you father Johnny and Arita. You worry unnecessarily, my love."

He grabbed her and swung her around in a circle, saying, "I am happier than I have ever been in my life. You, Maria, have brought so much joy to me, and I love you more for your gift, a Savory baby!"

Maria was overwhelmed with thoughts of what lay ahead, new husband, a man she adored and respected, two children she loved deeply, and now a new baby on the way. *Madre Mia, please guide me in this new journey of my life. Help me to adjust to constant interruptions and help me guide little Johnny and baby Arita. Give me the strength to carry this new baby and the patience to be a good helpmate for my dear husband. Thank you, heavenly Mother, for your son. Amen, and oh, I know that Mama Henrietta and Hanna will be here to comfort and encourage me whenever I need them. They have been sent to me from heaven to watch over me and my family. Amen, again!*

Hanna entered the teahouse from the back porch and saw Maria kneeling in prayer and waited until she was finished. Then she asked if the children could go with her to watch the fishermen come in. Maria looked at Hanna and smiled. Hanna looked at Maria and thought, *Maria give me feeling she is with child. Oh my! Betta tell Mama. Dis will make her berry happy. No, betta waits for Maria to tell 'bout da babee. Dis a very happy day, I tink.*

Seven months later, Albert Burbank Savory came into the world howling like a wolf at a full moon. Nathaniel was beside himself, yet he stayed a distance away. Arita, proud to be a big sister, could hardly wait to hold him. Johnny Boy just looked at him as a noisy pet. Mama Henrietta and Hanna were beside themselves with pride. The Savory line was established, and what a long line it would become.

Maria became pregnant before Albert was two months old. She was shocked, and Nathaniel was beside himself. He thought, *how can this be?* Albert was a few days shy of his first birthday when his sister Agnes came into their lives with a bang. Agnes stole her father's heart at once.

"Maria, she berry happy," Hanna announced, "but, Mistah Savory, he happy more. He all the time happy, he shua is, dis baby girl so purty, maka ever 'body happy."

This happiness would soon be shattered when Johnny Boy came upon his baby brother face down in a large puddle of water. "Mama,

Ma-ma!" Johnny shouted, as he ran to fetch help. "Mama! Albert, he in da wata by da tree, he not answer me, he jus' stay dea. Mama, please come, Albert not turn ova in da wata."

Maria, Hanna, and Johnny ran to the spot where Albert lay. Running as fast as she could, Maria knew when she first saw her baby that he was dead. She screamed out of pure pain, "Albert! Albert! Come to Mama!" Then a horrific scream escaped from her whole body. "Na-than-iel! Na-than-iel! She held her sweet little boy in her arms, rocking back and forth, saying, "Albert, tell Mommy what happened, please, please!"

Weeping, Hanna ran for Mama. "Sumting berry bad, berry bad, gotta find Mama!

Nathaniel heard the horrible scream from Maria and ran toward her voice. The scene that met him was one he would never forget.

Johnny ran up to him, saying, "Papa, sumting happen to Albert, help him, Papa."

Maria looked up at Nate, tears streaming down her face. "Albert won't wake up. Nate, make him wake up. Please, Nathaniel!"

Albert Burbank Savory was buried near their home the next day. Mama Henrietta helped Maria prepare him for burial. In the meantime, Nathaniel started looking into Albert's death and determined foul play.

After the burial, Mama did her own investigating and learned that a woman who Nathaniel lived with before he fell for Maria was suspect. Jealous of Maria for taking her man, so the rumor went. The woman was known to make threats at Maria, but never carrying them out. Mama Henrietta had no proof, so nothing came of it. No one ever knew what really happened to Albert. His mama and papa grieved for their firstborn.

Mama told Hanna, "Dey gotta have notha child, or dey will go mad, lika crazy man, no good to see, dey gotta git busy, make odda babee." Mama didn't know that Maria already carried another child.

Almost every year, Maria gave birth to a Savory baby. Her first was Albert, then Agnes, Caroline, Jane, Horace, Robert, Esther, and Benjamin. Baby Albert's drowning left Horace as the eldest Savory son.

Nathaniel, now almost seventy-five, sat in the old rocking chair on the back porch taking a siesta. After a while, he watched as Maria and two of their daughters gathered vegetables from the garden. He listened to their chatter as they moved up and down each row. *Ah, Maria knows so much about planting, the family will never want as long as she is around, what a blessed man I am.*

"Papa! Papa! Where you be? Papa!" shouted Horace Perry running through the teahouse yelling for his father.

"What do you want, Horace, why are you shouting like that?"

"Mama Henrietta, she go down to da ground real hard, she be out col', Papa. Come, we hafta help!"

Nathaniel shouted to Maria to follow him, and they hurried to Mama's side. Maria kept asking, "Why are we rushing so, Nathaniel? Is anything wrong at Mama's? Is she all right?"

Nathaniel walked as fast as he could, Maria taking four steps to his two. They came upon Hanna kneeling next to Mama, holding her hand, and crying. "Mama, mama, you be awright, you be awright." The native women stood shoulder to shoulder with worried faces, ready to help when they were asked.

Nathaniel knelt down at Henrietta's side and said, "Henrietta, Nate is here, let Maria, Hanna, and I take you to your home."

Mama opened her eyes and said, "Nathaniel, take Mama home, okay?"

As quick as a blink, the women formed a huge sling from the scarves they usually threw over their shoulders. Six women carried their beloved leader to her shanty—Maria, Hanna, Nathaniel, everyone walking alongside, moving carefully so as not to drop her.

Henrietta had suffered a stroke, which weakened her physical ability but surely not her ability to give orders, tell jokes, or give instructions. She lacked nothing; the love she projected to all was returned threefold. However, this incident gave her a start. She was getting older. She came to Bonin as one of the original settlers. She learned how to survive the hardships. Now she must prepare herself to go beyond, to meet her god.

One day, when Nathaniel visited her, Mama said, "Nathaniel, you an' me, we be friends long time, you a berry speshol man. I make a will fo' my two girls, Hanna and Maria, you do dis fo' me?

Nathaniel nodded to the affirmative. He couldn't speak as he became too emotional. He listened to everything Henrietta said without interruption.

She continued, "Hanna and Maria, dey mine, so da two of um, dey gonna haf my stuff wen I go to da odda place, you heah me, Nate? Maria, she marry good man, she haf you, but Hanna, no, so my stash goes to um, dey hafta make a decision ova what to do wid it."

"Okay? Fo' da burial, you make shua Mama be put in a proa on a soft mat wid me favorite quilt, in Henrietta's prettiest and best sarong, an' a lei of sweet-smelling flowers around me neck an' a crown of gardenias fo' me head…many flowers round da proa, fruits, an' vegetables to take wid me. Den you light fire on da proa an' push it way out ta sea, me knows God will be waiten' ta take me home wid him. Dat is me wish, so he'p to sign me X. Make dis plan da truth from Mama."

Proa at shoreline

"Wait a minute, Henrietta, what are you talking about? Ye ain't goin' nowhere, ye hear me. This talk! Ye will be here forever. No, I will not write your will!"

"Nathaniel, sumtime we hafta do wat we do not like, ye heah Mama, so ye betta he'p me, okay?"

Nathaniel, so upset, stomped off Henrietta's porch and practically ran up the mountain path, and at his age, not a wise thing to do.

He talked to himself, "That old womin, she sure is stubborn like a jackass. Write her will! By damn she sure knows how to git me goat, she does. Write her will, well, she ain't dying, no, she ain't. Knowing her like I do, she cain't, she hasta know everybody's business. How's she gonna do that if she's dead?" Nathaniel talking and answering himself continues, "Listen to you, Nathaniel, ye cain't make God's decisions. If God wants Henrietta now, he takes her. Talk about stubborn like an old donkey, let God decide. Betta writes her demands, I guess. Some woman…she sure can rile me dander up."

Life Goes On

THE *Portsmouth* arrived from Guam with a packet for the Savory family. The Spanish governor had issued them passports allowing them to return to Guam. Maria was shocked at this gesture after so many years of ignoring her.

"What? Nathaniel, tell them we do not accept their offer, not now and not later, no matter what they do. Give back the passports."

Nathaniel knew this would be her answer. No explanations needed, he had at first decided to keep the passports under lock and key until Maria asked for them.

Not in my lifetime, he thought. *Maria may never ask for them, so it's best I return these to Guam with a thank-you.*

One day, Hanna returned to her shanty with fresh vegetables from the garden and found Mama sleeping on the porch in her favorite chair, a rocking chair one of the sailors brought from China especially for her. Hanna quietly went about her business of cleaning and preparing the vegetables.

Hanna wasn't concerned at first, although Mama never ever took a siesta, so she went about doing her chores. Hanna had a strange feeling that this was not right and called Mama quite loud. No response. She then rushed to the chair and started to shake Mama. No response. Hanna began to cry quietly at first, still calling Mama's name, "Mama, Mama. No, no, no, Henrietta, wake up, you not go now. No, no, no!"

Hanna's painful screams could be heard throughout the village, even up to the hills. Nathaniel had a strange feeling of loss even though he did not know why. Maria, moving about the garden, heard the soulful cry coming from the village, and somehow, she knew who it came from. She knew and began to run toward the sound.

One of the Kanaka men pulled the conch shell from its place of honor and blew to the god of heavens, the gods of the sea, and the wind telling them that Henrietta, loved by everyone, was on her way home. The mournful sound of the conch was heard far out to sea and high in the sky. Hearing the sound, it alerted the fishermen to return to shore. The mourning villagers began their journey to say and sing their good-byes to the beloved woman.

Maria, even though she was very pregnant, ran to Mama's side and knelt beside her body, weeping for this wonderful woman who mothered her through so much. Nathaniel, tears sitting precariously in his eyes, walked slowly through the crowds and enveloped the sobbing Maria and Hanna in his arms.

Finally, he chokingly said, "We must prepare her for burial."

Hanna, Maria, and two of the women who were close to Henrietta started the preparation for the burial. Maria and Hanna followed Mama's instruction as to what she would wear and how her hair would be fashioned. Some of the other women began the task of weaving some of the items Henrietta would take on her journey to the other side. Others prepared the feast to be served after Mama's proa sailed away, and others did their part in picking the flowers to be used in the making of some leis. The men guided by Nathaniel prepared the proa just as Mama had asked. Nothing would be left out. Henrietta would be pleased. Even Agnes, still a young girl, took charge of the older siblings while Arita took the youngest, giving their parents the time to honor the woman they knew only as Mama. Johnny went with Nathaniel to assist wherever he was needed.

Once the preparations were complete, Maria and Hanna stood quietly at Henrietta's resting place as all the villagers…yes, even some of the castaway sailors walked past to pay their respects and say a final good-bye.

The next morning, Nathaniel, Johnny, and several of the fishermen walked the bier down to the water and placed Henrietta's body into the proa exactly as she requested. Behind Henrietta's body, lovingly carried, a procession with the entire village followed behind Maria, Hanna, and the Savory children.

Mama was dressed in her prettiest and best sarong with the beautiful leis of sweet-smelling flowers the women placed around her neck and a crown of flowers for her long, flowing hair. The women scattered flowers of every kind plus fruit and vegetables in the proa for her journey. She looked like a queen, a beautiful, loving woman looking toward the end of her journey.

Two proa-like canoes sailed up to sandwich the funeral bier between them—Nathaniel in one with an oarsman, and another oarsman and the conch blower in the other. All four men were dressed in leis. Nathaniel held a long paddle as if it were a scepter, and it too was encircled with vines and flowers. The two canoes pulled the funeral bier with braided hemp ropes out through the breakwater. Soon the two canoe escorts pulled Henrietta's bier up to and just past them. Nathaniel torched the canoe; then with the paddle and all his strength, he pushed the burning canoe out to the deepest water. Nathaniel, tears streaming from his eyes, shouted at the burning canoe, "Go in peace, beloved and dear friend." The four islanders sat a time as they watched the fire engulf their beloved friend then rowed sadly back to shore.

In tradition of the islands they originally came from, bonfires were lit up and down the shoreline, as the drums began the somber sound, *Arum! Arum! Arum!* A slow hypnotic beat, then the humming of a chant from the men then the women. Soon the beat became faster and louder. The chanting grew as the drumbeat grew and finished together in a dramatic climax.

Someone strummed a familiar song to all on a ukulele, a song Henrietta had enjoyed singing. Into the night the wake continued. Fish, rice, fruits, vegetables passed around in celebration of Henrietta's life with them. Many funny stories were told about her, and this day and night they knew Henrietta was right up there looking down on them and smiling.

The Miracle

HEAVINESS cloaked the island for weeks after Mama Henrietta died. Nothing could shake the pain of their loss. Mama was their spark, she ignited their spirit, and now she is no more.

Nathaniel thought, *If the Bonin people do not shake this dark feeling, they would waste away. How can I stave off this travesty? Only a miracle could help them now.*

Work went on, but there was no energy; they were spiritless. The islanders needed something to look forward to or something to jar them from their morose, as Henrietta did. Nathaniel was worried for the people, they were not many in number, but still this grief blanketed the whole community, literally bringing it to a halt.

Spontaneously Nathaniel heard himself praying, "Dear God, I have been a lost son, but I have seen the work that you do, and now dear Father, I am praying for your intervention in the troubles of our wonderful people, they are your sons and daughters too. It would devastate your daughter Henrietta, who believed and loved you true, if she were to see how her families on earth have chosen to let her dying destroy their spirit, she'd be unhappy and sad for the islanders. Help me, Father, to move them forward as Henrietta would do. I need your guidance, Father, please intervene." Tears streamed down Nathaniel's face, as he and Maria grieved the loss of this remarkable woman as well. He was not used to praying and asking for something. Little did Nathaniel know, God was already answering his prayer.

Hanna and Maria kept busy in their garden. They spoke about Mama often and laughed at some of the things she did and said. This was their way of grieving. Mama loved the children and Maria wanted them to remember her, not with sadness but with joy. This was their way of honoring their surrogate mother and grandmother. There were six children now, and Maria was pregnant with her seventh due at any time.

Maria would never forget Mama's kindnesses. When she needed someone to help her get through the nightmare of the earlier days under Mazarro, Mama and Hanna played a big part in her survival. Henrietta became her comforter. She and Hanna became Maria's closest friends, her adopted family, during those early days. How lucky she was to meet these two women.

Both Hanna and Maria decided that they would try to comfort the small group of natives, both of them working with one family at a time. The two women knew that it would be a slow process but one that was badly needed. They started with one of the families. They were strong and hearty men, along with their women and children lived off the sea, and they knew what tragedy was. Somehow, the loss of Henrietta was different. She took the role of nurturer, comforter, and leader. Who will fill that role for them? However, they believed in God and his ways. With Henrietta, they loved her as if she were their own. They grieved silently for her. Maria knew all of these families, but she was not sure if they would accept her help. She went anyway. Moreover, they showed her respect, not because she was Nathaniel's wife, but because of her strength.

After the visits to each of the families, things began to change. One by one, they sought the sea, and fishing became their solace. One day, George, out fishing, paddled back to shore in a great rush. He pulled his boat up onto the sand and began to yell, "Someone git Mistah Savory an' hurry. Bring him heah fast he gotta see dis!"

Nathaniel hurried to the shore and saw a strange sight—a black ship. He cleaned the spyglass to see more clearly, and what he saw was a black American warship belching white smoke and in the sea breeze the Stars and Stripes whipping in the wind.

Nathaniel was beside himself with emotion seeing the flag of his country. Oh, he had seen the American flag flying above the whaling ships, but he knew this was different. He'd been waiting almost twenty-five years for the United States to recognize the island of Bonin, and now they are here. *Thank the good Father above,* he prayed silently. *Today is an auspicious day, Nathaniel,* he thought to himself, as he waited for the dingy to come on shore. *Who could the captain be? By the looks of him, he is no lowly salt. Wondah what brings them here?*

June 14, 1853, a big day for the Boninites. The villagers stopped everything they were doing and lined the waterfront, silently watching as the small flotilla of boats rowed slowly toward shore. One man stood, in formal navy dress, at the bow of the first dingy. Nathaniel stood at the landing place and waited for it to reach shore.

A young lieutenant approached the group watching the boats land and asked to speak to the person in charge. In a chorus-like response, they shouted over the noise of the surf and the ship "Mistah Savory is dah man to speak to," pointing toward Nathaniel. The young lieutenant acknowledged that he saw Nathaniel and headed toward him.

"Ah, Mr. Savory, good morning, sir," reaching out his hand. "I am Lieutenant Pickham, pleased to meet you, sir. I serve on the USS Susquehanna.

USS Susquehanna

My captain has sent me ahead to request permission for our ships to anchor in your beautiful harbor. We sail under the command of Commodore Mathew Perry of the United States Navy. May we come ashore, sir, for a few days? We have two ships with us, sir, our flagship, the steam-assisted *Susquehanna* and the *Mississippi*, which will be here within an hour or two. Upon leaving your harbor, we will return to the rest of our fleet, currently visiting Shanghai."

Still in a state of euphoric shock upon seeing the warships for the first time and the fact they were American, he pinched himself to make sure he wasn't dreaming and welcomed the young lieutenant then invited the group to come onto the island.

"Thank you, sir, I shall report your invitation to my superior, and we will start debarking right away."

He snapped to attention, saluted Nathaniel, and returned to the dingy with the invitation for Commodore Perry to come ashore.

After the formal introductions, Nathaniel invited Commodore Perry to the teahouse for refreshments. Commodore Perry instructed the lieutenant to keep the men on shore until he returned; then he turned to Nathaniel as they walked toward the teahouse.

"I am quite surprised to find you, an American. Have you been on this island long, Mr. Savory?"

"Let me see, I been here on Bonin since 1830 or thereabouts, 'bout twenty-three years, was still a young man of twenty-plus years," Nathaniel responded. "Best thing I ever did."

Nathaniel asked why the American warships were in the area, especially here in the area of Bonin.

Susquehanna crew relax at the river

Mr. Perry explained that the United States was surveying the Orient, and after they docked in Shanghai, he decided to leave three of his ships in the Chinese port while the *Susquehanna* and the *Mississippi* followed a whaling map on the northwestern side of this group of islands to see if exploration was possible. They were under the assumption that this island was uninhabited, and much to their surprise, they found people living here.

"Well, Commodore, we ain't many but do pretty well, long as we have the whalers, we keep mighty busy."

Just then, Agnes, Nathaniel, and Maria's eldest daughter entered the room. "Agnes, this is Commodore Perry from the United States, they'll be here as our guests, fetch us the tea, girl, and tell yer Ma to come in."

Agnes brought in the mugs of rum, and Nathaniel raised his to the commodore and said, "To the Blessed Almighty who brought ye to us, I pray welcome, mate. Mighty good to see you, sir. Now what can this little island do for you?"

A very pregnant Maria came into the teahouse and stood quietly until Nate saw her. "Oh, wonderful, I take great pleasure in introducing my beautiful wife and mother of our brood. Mr. Commodore, me wife, Maria Da Los Santos y Castro Savory. She hails from the island of Guam."

Commodore Perry bowed and said, "Your husband is a lucky man, madam, it is my pleasure to meet you. Thank you for your hospitality."

Maria nodded her acknowledgement to this man and noticed how excited and proud Nate was when the commodore was introduced. *Nate has waited so long for someone like this stranger, a man of authority from the United States. Maybe his prayers will be answered. This man must be very important to excite Nathaniel like this,* she thought.

The commodore and Nathaniel met for quite a while. In their discussions, the commodore asked permission to send a party inland to survey the interior for scientific purposes. And he was interested in surveying the land bordering the harbor, asking Nathaniel to be his guide. The purpose for the survey was to see if the island had coal. Mr. Perry explained that the future of the seagoing vessels will rely on coal to support the new steamships being built today and that all of his present fleet was fueled with coal.

Nathaniel, impressed with what he heard, gladly took Mr. Perry on a tour of the land, especially situated by the harbor. This was Savory land, and the two men negotiated a purchase price of fifty acres of prime land adjacent to the harbor for $50.

Mr. Perry took a great interest in Bonin, especially Port Lloyd. The harbor is deep and quite capable of holding several ships.

Nathaniel responded that the inland survey would be a good start to learn about the topography. If there were scientists aboard, they certainly should take some samples to study. This had not been done before, and the outcome could serve a good purpose for the island.

With this gentleman's agreement, Nathaniel queried, "Mr. Perry, sir, are you planning on acquiring this island for the United States as it is of British possession, although England has never acknowledged the fact? If you are, then, you, sir, are an answer to my prayer since I landed here over two decades ago. I have prayed to have the United States fly the Stars 'n' Stripes, and you can make it happen."

While the two parties—one going to the south, the other traveling inland—were surveying the island, Commodore Perry and Nathaniel were negotiating the price of an additional parcel of land fronting the Ten Fathom Hole. Commodore Perry purchased the land with the idea that a coaling station could be established to fuel the new era of steamships in the near future.

Perry presented Nathaniel with the American flag, which Nathaniel proudly flew over the teahouse. Later that day, the two survey parties returned with sufficient information regarding the terrain and animal inhabitants. Perry announced to Nathaniel, "We succeeded with our initial mission, and it is time for us to bid farewell."

The next morning, the harbor pilot guided first the *Mississippi* safely out of the harbor, followed by the *Susquehanna*, black smoke belching from her smokestack. With a long blast from the ships' horn as a final good-bye, they sailed out of sight of those watching from shore.

Maria, standing silently next to Nathaniel with the new baby in her arms, looked up at Nathaniel and asked, "Do you think America will come back, my husband?"

"I hope so, my love, I hope so!"

Epilogue

T HE visit of Commodore Matthew Perry and his black steamship of war was without a doubt one of the highlights of Nathaniel's self-imposed exile to the Bonin Islands. Probably his greatest disappointment—America never came back. Although extremely proud of his American roots, he never went back but kept in touch with his brothers and sisters through letters and messages sent via the many whalers leaving the New Bedford shores for the whaling fields. The gift of the American flag began a tradition for him and his boys. At sundown every day, one of his sons, standing at attention, would ceremoniously retire the flag; next morning at dawn, Nathaniel would raise the Stars and Stripes.

Japan decided to reestablish its ownership of the islands in 1875, and on their arrival, the Japanese brought with them a small group of people who established a village on Bonin. The British had given up their rights of ownership. This could have been disastrous, but the Boninites, led by Savory, was able to accept the Japanese without prejudice. Each of them lived peacefully in separate villages.

Nathaniel Savory died peacefully in 1874 at age eighty in his island home with those he loved. Nathaniel and Maria parented ten children. One of their daughters, Helen Jane, married Davis Webb, whose father settled in Bonin several years after the first group arrived. Alice, one of the Webb daughters, while attending school in Yokohama, met and fell in love with and married a Spanish sea captain from Guam, Vicente P. Herrero. My mother, Lillian Julia, was one of their six children. Thus, Nathaniel and Maria are my great-great-grandparents.

As a child living in Guam, I remember my grandparents, Vincente and Jane, as well as Papa and Mama Herrero. I remember Mama Herrero traveling by ship very often to Japan and throughout the Orient to visit her family. She died from cancer in 1936. Her story and that of the many Savory descendants, some of whom still call Bonin (Ogasawara) home, can tell you many stories of change in their lives even today in the twenty-first century.

Our families, those of the Alice Webb and Vicente P. Herrero, have a shared heritage of exciting and wonderful stories, made possible by adventurers who explored the Pacific in the seventeenth, eighteenth, and nineteenth centuries. My brother, sisters, and I can relive these historical events through stories passed down by our parents who learned of them through their parents. The trials and tribulations of Maria Del Los Santos y Duarte, how her aunt selfishly duped her, how Nathaniel Savory became an integral part of our lives, and many more wonderful stories about these two extraordinary people. How the adventures of Nathaniel Savory and the sad events of Maria's life came to form part of who we, as a family, are today.

The stories I grew up hearing as we sat around the Sunday dinner table, through my father's interpretation of the facts as he heard them, were fascinating to me. I had never heard of the island of Bonin until my dad began to tell us about the place where Mama Herrero was born, how she met our Papa, and the stories of Papa's sailing days as captain of his own ship, bringing commerce to Guam. Our dad was a wonderful storyteller. I lived every story, every adventure.

I grew up knowing that I wanted to become the storyteller for my children, to write about the remarkable people who gave us life. What do we have now? My husband and I have twenty grandchildren asking for these same stories of me.